WEST AGAINST
THE WIND

WEST AGAINST THE WIND

Liza Ketchum Murrow

HOLIDAY HOUSE / NEW YORK

Library of Congress Cataloging-in-Publication Data

Murrow, Liza Ketchum
   West against the wind.

   Summary: Fourteen-year-old Abby seeks both her father and the secret of a handsome but mysterious boy
during an arduous journey by wagon train from the middle of the country to the Pacific coast in 1850.
   [1. Frontier and pioneer life—Fiction] I. Title.
PZ7.M96713We 1987   [Fic]   87-45337
ISBN 0-8234-0668-7

For Casey, Derek, and Ethan

WEST AGAINST
THE WIND

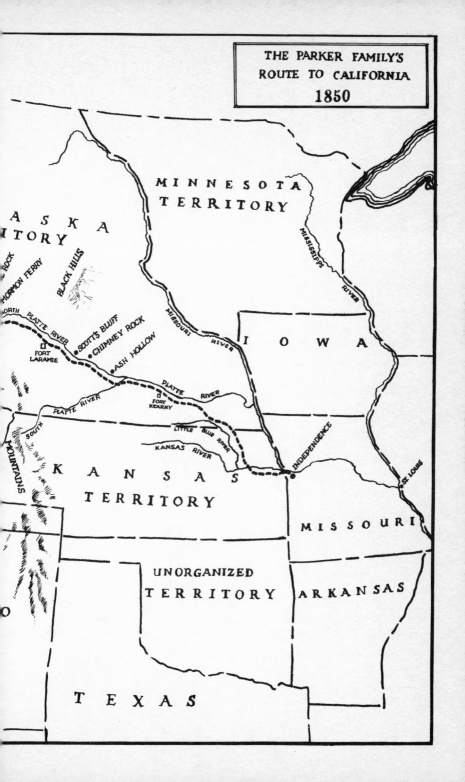

THE PARKER FAMILY'S
ROUTE TO CALIFORNIA
1850

April 29, 1850. Independence, Missouri.

In the cold, thin light before sunup, a circle of wagons loomed like sleeping elephants in the mist. Fog crept in heavy coils off the Missouri River, shrouding the campground. Abby stood still in a grove of cottonwood trees. The clouds would hide her as she came out into the open, and the sound of the river would muffle her footsteps. She bent to pick up a heavy crate and edged slowly toward the wagons.

She passed her family's oxen, huddled with lowered heads, their bodies lost in fog. A tethered pony whickered softly. "Quiet, Timothy," Abby said. "Don't wake them. I don't have much time." The pony nuzzled her pockets and turned away to pick at the trampled grass.

Her thoughts ran on ahead of her. What if she couldn't finish the job before dawn? Or worse, what if Uncle Joseph woke and found her? She hoped the fog would hold, as it had other mornings, causing everyone to sleep past first light.

Abby set the crate down beside her family's supply wagon, parked at some distance from the circle. She crouched beneath it and felt about in the shadows until her hands gripped a hidden can. Nothing moved; everyone was silent, sleeping beneath an orderly row of tents and canvas shelters. A flock of geese rose from the river with beating wings and flew overhead. Abby watched them fly west. We'll follow soon, she thought, and her stomach quivered. She had to hurry. She stepped onto the overturned crate, which wobbled for a moment, then steadied.

Abby held up the can, hoping her uncle wouldn't need it that morning. She pulled her father's knife from her apron pocket and pried open the lid. Thick, black axle grease oozed across her fingers. She drew a slab of wood from the same deep pocket, dipped the stick gingerly into the can of grease, and scooped out a heavy dollop of sticky paste. Reaching high onto the side of the wagon, she drew the grease down the osnaburg cover. The faint odor of linseed oil in the canvas mingled with the smell of tar as Abby pushed the stick down, then up, down and up again, to form the letter W.

As she worked, Abby listened to the deep song of the current sweeping past the campground. Mother had bought her a diary here in Independence. Abby had privately named the small leather book her "river scrapbook." In it she would record all the rivers and streams they crossed, from the Missouri to the Yuba in California.

She was so absorbed in drawing her crude letters that she didn't notice the sun creep up over the murky river in a white ball that dissolved the fog.

A stick snapped. Abby froze, then turned slowly to peer into the shadows. The budding cottonwoods arched over the figure of a man. Abby held her breath. Had Will discovered her? No, this person was too tall and bony to be her brother, and the cumbersome pack at his feet must mean he was a stranger. Abby couldn't see his face beneath the crumpled hat, and something in his stillness, the way his hands hung loose at his sides, made her feel he'd been watching her for some time. She gripped the can of grease.

"Good morning." The man touched his hat and stepped toward her. "Looks as though I've stumbled on the camp artist."

His voice was friendly, and Abby decided, after a closer look, that he was only a few years older than she was. His face was smooth, with a faint bristle of hair above the upper lip. She relaxed her grip on the can and whispered, "Hello."

He smiled and drew closer, pushing back his hat. A shock of loose, sandy hair fell down onto his forehead. "Looks as though you're pretty busy," he said. "Mind if I watch?"

"If you're quiet. I don't want to wake anyone." Abby began to work again, but it was awkward, trying to paint while he stood there, his head cocked to one side. "What do you want?" she asked. "Are you looking for someone?"

"Not exactly." He hesitated, and seemed to measure his words. "I'm hoping to find a family that needs a hired hand."

Abby studied him a minute before painting another letter. She liked his quick smile and the way his gray eyes changed color in the light. But he might be a runaway; she'd known boys at home in Ohio who disappeared—the promise of gold sucked them away.

"I don't know," she said. "You'd have to ask Mr. Foster. He's our captain."

"You're headed for California?"

"Yes." Abby wished he would go away. The sun was up now; she had to hurry.

"When do you leave?" the young man asked.

"Today or tomorrow," Abby whispered. "Why don't you find the captain? He decides when the trail is dry and when there's enough grass for the oxen."

"I'm going to California too," he said. He didn't seem to notice her impatience. "I started out with my father." He looked down and scuffed the dirt with his boot. "He's gone now."

Abby painted two more letters and then peered into his face, which was shadowed by the brown hat. "What happened to him?" she asked.

He cleared his throat. There was a catch in his voice, and she had to lean over to hear him.

"He died on the boat, just before we landed. I promised him I wouldn't give up—that is, that I'd keep on to California, as we planned. When we came ashore, I buried him."

Abby recoiled a little. She had heard about sickness on the riverboats that came down the Great Lakes and the Illinois River loaded with men. The travelers slept stacked on shelves like bags of grain, and the boats pulled into the dock "steaming with cholera"—that's how Uncle Joseph put it.

Was that how this man's father had died? Abby was afraid to ask and moved to the edge of the crate, to put some distance between them. Then she noticed sorrow flickering in his eyes. "I'm sorry," she said.

He nodded. Abby didn't know what else to say, so she returned to her work, thinking about the day Pa left, just a year ago. He'd stood in front of her, his eyes dry, though rimmed with red. "Put out your hands," he said, after she hugged him goodbye, and he placed his worn knife in one outstretched palm, his heavy pocket-watch in the other.

"Every girl needs a knife," he had said. "And the watch will help you keep track of the time—until I'm with you again." Then he kissed her forehead, tickling her cheeks with his red beard, embraced her mother and sister—and was gone.

As she painted, Abby felt the watch tick close to her throat. For twelve long months, it had been her talisman; her good-luck charm. What if Pa were gone forever, like this man's father? She wrote the letter A and turned around.

"My father went out with the Gold Rush last spring," Abby said. "Just after he arrived, he wrote and told us to come. We haven't heard anything since, and we don't really know where he is."

Abby stopped. Why wouldn't he look at her?

"What's your name?" she asked.

"Matthew Reed here, at your service, ma'am," he said, and swept off his hat to make a low mock bow from the waist.

Abby laughed. She didn't know what to make of him. One minute he seemed miserable, and the next instant he was poking fun at her—or at himself.

"What's *your* name?" he asked.

"Abigail Parker. Or Abby."

"Well, Abigail, or Abby, what do you think? Would your family take me on?"

Abby considered him again. He was spare-looking and lanky —"in need of a bath and a clean shirt," Mother might say. His hands looked deeply callused, as if he might be a good worker; Uncle Joseph would like that. Still, he seemed a little secretive—about himself, and his father's death.

"Look as long as you like," Matthew said. "I don't mind."

Abby turned away quickly. She could never control the blush that rose from her neck up into her cheeks. Even without a mirror, she knew her freckles would deepen to bronze, until they almost matched her hair. "I don't know," she said, trying to sound distant. "You'd have to ask Uncle Joseph. Or my mother. I'm sure my brother Will would be glad to have you." She scooped one last dollop of grease and slapped it onto the canvas.

"There!" she said and stepped down from the crate to

admire the full length of the sign, which wavered and scrawled its way across the wagon cover.

"William G. Parker Family. Ho for California!" Matthew read aloud. He laughed. "I guess everyone will know who you are. Is that what you want?"

Abby thought of all the other wagons, with bold elephants, wolves, and eagles emblazoned on canvas or slogans scrawled along the side. "I thought we needed something to make us stand out a little," she said, though this was not the whole truth. In fact, she worried that Pa might be headed back east. If he hadn't received their letter saying they were coming, he might have decided to return home. Any day he could pass them in the crowds—unless he saw his own name painted in bold letters on the wagon cover.

Abby jammed the lid back on the grease can and shoved it under the wagon. The campground was waking up around them; chickens clucked nearby and men moved about under the trees. Smoke from campfires filtered through the misty sunlight. "I've got to find our cow," Abby said. "And I don't want my family to know what I've been doing. Uncle Joseph and Aunt Emma sleep there"—she pointed to her uncle's wagon. "That's Mother's, beside it. And Will sleeps in that tent. They'll be up before long."

Before Matthew could answer, Abby ran to the edge of the river, where she knelt in the soft gravel, rubbing gritty sand across her palms. She scrubbed her hands in the icy water until the grease faded to gray stains. What would Uncle Joseph say to Matthew? He complained about women coming along, so he might be glad of a man's help. On the other hand, he worried about the wagons being overloaded. But it was not long since his first wife and baby had died. He might feel a spark of sympathy for a young man traveling alone, without a family.

Matthew was the least of her problems. What would happen when Uncle Joseph saw her sign? He was so proud of his new supply wagon, which he'd bought in Independence to ease the crowded conditions they'd felt traveling from Ohio. He boasted about its sturdy frame, the four new oxen he'd found to pull it, the size of the wagon box beneath the seat. Abby had helped Mother oil the lofty cover—and now she'd spoiled it.

She hurried back to the campground, weaving through small clusters of men and animals. The stench of uncovered latrines, rotten food, and garbage mixed with the acrid smell of wet, burning wood. Abby covered her mouth with one hand and ran to her wagon.

Mother stood over the fire, making corn cakes. Even this early in the morning, she had coiled her dark hair neatly on top of her head. Somehow, the faded calico dress that hugged her worn, spare figure managed to look neat after days of wear. How did she do it? Aunt Emma always looked clean too, Abby thought, and elegant, besides. Abby knew her own russet-colored hair was disheveled this morning, and the hem of her dress was sodden from the mud on the riverbank. She tried to slip into the wagon without her mother seeing her, but Mary Parker raised her head.

"Abigail! Where have you been?" she asked. "You need to milk Suzy. We have a day's packing ahead of us. I expect you to do your chores early in the morning."

"I'm sorry, Mother. I'll be right out." She started to ask about Matthew Reed but decided it was better not to mention him yet. She didn't want Mother to know she'd made friends with a total stranger this morning. Instead, she climbed up over the tall wheel and into the wagon. It rocked gently, then steadied.

It was dim inside, with the cover closed. Every inch of space was filled with belongings, and Abby had to crawl along the mattress she shared with Mother to reach her trunk. As she leaned across the narrow bed, she noticed a folded letter poking out from beneath the quilt. She picked it up and peered through the slit in the canvas. The fire blazed, but Mother was not in sight. Maybe she was talking to Matthew Reed.

Abby knelt on the mattress and unfolded the creased sheets of paper. Her hands trembled. She had never read this letter, though Mother often referred to it. It was the only one Pa had sent. Abby remembered how Pa laughed when he packed the pen and paper Mother insisted on giving him. "Don't expect many letters, Mary," he laughed. "You know me. But I'll miss you and think of you, just the same."

Abby waited for her eyes to adjust to the light and began to read. The first part told about the trip across plains, mountains, and deserts. Then her father described the constant winter rains, the snow in the mountains of California, and the illnesses that seemed to strike everyone around him. "I'm just too busy to get sick," he said.

Abby read eagerly, looking up now and then to make sure she was still alone. On the next page, Pa wrote:

Mary, I want you to come and join me. There's money in the streams, and even more to be made supplying the miners. Sell the farm, and leave the store for Jacob and Caroline. You'll need a good sum of money to outfit yourselves, and more for the journey itself.

Bring the family. There's something here for all of us. The country is full of promise. Mary, I don't want to come home. Think of it—no more hard winters or failed crops! Once this rough crowd gets civilized, it will be a good life.

I've written to Joseph, to suggest he might join you. He could forget the past here, make a fresh start. Perhaps he should find a bride first—women are few and far between.

Leave as early in the spring as the wagons can move. It's a long, rough journey, but I know you can make it. You and Abigail are stronger than most women. Join with a big company, for safety's sake.

Abby continued through detailed advice about what to bring, what to leave behind. Pa mentioned detours and advised his wife to travel over Truckee Pass—"Don't listen to anyone else. It's the fastest way to the Yuba River. That's where I'll wait for you."

Abby blushed when she came to the next paragraph. This must be why Mother kept the letter hidden.

Mary, my dearest, in spite of the wonders of the gold country, I miss you terribly, and can never fall asleep at night without seeing your sweet face and wishing for the comfort of your touch....

There was more, but Abby quickly folded the letter and shoved it back beneath the quilt.

"William!" Uncle Joseph's voice boomed across the campground. "Did you decide to decorate the wagon last night?"

Abby couldn't hear her brother's reply. She stepped out to the rim of the wheel, spread her arms, and jumped down. She crept to the supply wagon, where she found Mother, Will, and her aunt Emma standing with their backs to her, the women's faces hidden by their sunbonnets. Matthew Reed shifted uneasily from one foot to the other at the far end of the wagon; he threw Abby a distant, puzzled look. Abby started to smile, then looked away. He's pretending he doesn't know me, she thought.

Uncle Joseph stood with his legs apart, his tall boots planted in the wet grass and his hands on his hips. He thrust his chin forward at Will until his beard almost bristled. Like a bear, Abby thought, suppressing a giggle. An angry bear.

Uncle Joseph drew his dark eyebrows together and scowled. "Well, who would paint our wagon, without permission?" he demanded.

"I would." Abby stepped forward into the little circle. There was a stunned silence, and she forced herself to keep talking as cheerfully as she could. "Good morning, everyone. How do you like my sign?"

"Not a bit," said Uncle Joseph. His brown eyes grew almost black as they receded into their sockets. "I might have known it was you. Your mother promised you'd behave on this trip. 'Almost a grown woman,' she said. More like a child, I'd say. What explanation do you have for yourself?"

Out of the corner of her eye, Abby saw Mother's back stiffen. Now she was angry, too. Would this mean more trouble?

"Listen to me, Abigail," her uncle was saying. "You used a full can of grease. I expect you to replace it. As for the sign"—he pointed to the name William—"you might have been courteous enough to include the Joseph Parker family. Who bought this wagon, I'd like to know?"

Abby's stomach churned. She'd never thought of writing her uncle's name. She knew her tone was rude, but she couldn't help it. "I'm sorry, Uncle. I could paint your name on the other side, if you like." Uncle Joseph's face was almost purple; Abby knew hers must be a deep copper.

"Joseph. Abigail. Please." Mary Parker spoke softly but firmly. "It seems to me this is not such a crime. Many wagons have signs. Just look around. And none of us will get lost, with the Parker name painted so boldly."

Abby longed to thank her mother for understanding, but she didn't dare interrupt.

"It's just a case of gold rush fever," Mother continued. "You're a victim yourself, aren't you?"

"He is, he is," said Aunt Emma, speaking for the first time. "He's got a terrible case of it. Look at the gleam in his eyes." Abby thought her aunt winked at her, but it passed so quickly, she couldn't be sure.

Mother went on in her most reasonable voice. "Please, Joseph. Forget about the sign; it will wash off eventually. There's something more important to consider: how we get this extra wagon to California. Meet Matthew Reed. He's a nice young man, traveling alone, good with oxen. Could we sign him on as a hired hand?" She motioned to Matthew, who stepped forward into their circle.

Abby was relieved that someone else was the center of attention. Matthew Reed held out his hand to Uncle Joseph, who shook it quickly and then stamped his foot in disgust.

"You women certainly know how to complicate things, don't you?" Uncle Joseph asked. "I don't know that we need any help. What do you think, Will?"

Will looked at Matthew and then back at his uncle. He shrugged his shoulders. "Well, we made it all right from home," he said. "But I did wonder who would drive the third wagon."

"I expect everyone will drive," Mary Parker answered, to Abby's surprise. "Even so, we might appreciate an extra pair of hands."

Uncle Joseph threw up his arms. "Leave now, all of you. I'll talk to Mr. Reed in private. We can't take on a total stranger without thinking carefully. We have our own needs to consider. What are you waiting for?" he shouted when no one moved. "The animals are hungry, and so am I. There's packing to do. We leave tomorrow."

"Go on, Will, Abigail," Mother said. "Help Emma with breakfast. We need more wood, and the cow's waiting. I'll be with you in a moment."

She must mean to plead Matthew's case, Abby thought. I wonder if he mentioned anything about his father. Well, he kept my painting a secret, so I'll have to keep quiet about his father's death and hope we don't all catch cholera. And Matthew never mentioned the Gold Rush. Why does he want to go west alone, when he could go home?

She wouldn't think about that now. Whatever happened to Matthew, her own journey would begin tomorrow. They were headed for California—and the Yuba River—at last.

May 1, 1850. Leaving the Missouri River.

Dearest Caroline,
We're off to California! The captain came before dawn
yesterday to tell us the trail was ready. We forgot about

breakfast, as we rushed to fit everything in for the last time. The wagons are bursting!

We joined with a company of ten wagons. I had hoped for another girl to talk to, but Mother, Emma, and I are the only women. There are more animals than people. We have the horses, of course, the cow, and now a cage full of chickens. Mother bought them in Independence and tied them to the back of our wagon. You can imagine what Uncle Joseph says about that!

Uncle Joseph sold our mules and bought oxen. They're clumsy, but he says they'll eat anything, and they're strong. The men manage them with big bull-whips. Will thinks he has to crack ours all the time, now he's learned.

We have a new wagon, and a new hired man to drive it. His name is Matthew Reed. He knows more about oxen than any of us, and he's glad to travel with a family. (I have to admit he's more pleasing to look at than Orly Green back home!)

Mr. Colt, a man traveling with us, has cholera. It's everywhere, Mother says. There's a noisy, rough man in the company—a Mr. Grey—who told the captain to abandon Mr. Colt. Mother was shocked. She's given the man medicine, but he's no better today. Of course, no one else wanted to leave the poor man behind.

We've left the Missouri River now. I plan to keep track of all the rivers and streams between here and California. I thought of swimming in every one, but so far it's too cold and rainy—even for me.

We walked all day beside the wagons, and now I'm

spattered with mud. Mother wants me to fetch water for dinner, so I will run and be first to see what this next stream looks like. Dear sister, do you suppose we'll ever see each other again? Kiss my nephew for me, and tell him his aunt Abby is far away, bouncing through the mud in a covered wagon, looking for his grandpa.

Love from your affectionate sister,
Abigail

May 5. Near the Wakarusa River, west of Independence.

Rain fell steadily on the covered wagons, which lurched and struggled through mud and deep ruts. Abby sat on the mattress and peered out on the snaking line of travelers. The straggling parade stretched ahead to the gray horizon and behind her as far as she could see. Abby sighed and pulled her diary from her trunk. "Wakarusa River," she wrote. The pen slid across the page as the oxen churned through another rut. "Swollen and muddy. Crossed at noon."

It was too rough to write. Abby replaced the diary in her trunk and looked for a familiar face among the travelers walking nearby. She recognized Frank Watson, a young man who came to share stories and songs with

Will and Matthew some evenings, but her family was nowhere in sight. She hadn't seen her mother since they crossed the river; she must be with Mr. Colt, the man with cholera.

The wagon shuddered and jolted to a stop. As she pulled open the cover, Abby saw Matthew jump down from the wagon behind her. His hat and coat were soaked from the rain. "Abby!" he called. "Hold the oxen. I'll go see what's wrong."

Abby climbed down and dodged the ruts, her skirts held high. She stood beside the wet animals, soothing them quietly. Clouds of steam billowed from their wet backs.

In a few minutes, Matthew returned, looking grim.

"What happened?" Abby asked.

"Mr. Colt's dead. And a wagon from another company tipped over. No one's hurt, but they broke an axle. Trying to beat us to the Gold Fields, I suppose." He gave her a weak smile, but he looked worried.

"Trying to escape cholera, *I* think," said Abby. "Is that how your father died?"

"No." Matthew pulled his hat down and turned away.

"Matthew. I promise I won't tell anyone—"

"He *didn't* have cholera!" Matthew hissed.

"Sorry," Abby said, but she wondered if he was telling the truth. Rain fell in thin sheets around them, filling the ruts with brown rivulets. She shivered. "What about Mr. Colt? Will they bury him here?"

Matthew nodded. "Your uncle and the captain are the

only ones who offered to help his brother dig the grave. And your uncle's worried—Emma's gone off somewhere."

"I'll look for her," Abby said. She was relieved to leave and pick her way to Uncle Joseph's wagon. She didn't know her new aunt very well yet. She and Uncle Joseph had only been married a few months when Uncle Joseph decided to go west. Abby knew that Emma had begged him to stay in Ohio. "Please, don't make me leave my mother," Emma had said. "She's all the family I have."

"You have a new family now," Uncle Joseph said, and that was the end of it. Abby jumped a puddle between the two wagons and almost fell over her aunt, who stood huddled next to the front wheel. Rain dripped from her bonnet onto her dark shawl.

"Aunt Emma—you're so wet!" Abby cried. "You'll catch cold. Come into the wagon with me."

Aunt Emma turned her large, dark eyes on Abby. "Oh, Abigail, it's miserable. First the rain, now a death. I don't know if I can bear it. Joseph's gone to help with the burial. What if he catches cholera?"

What if Mother does? Abby wondered. "Don't worry," she said aloud, trying to sound cheerful. "I'm sure he'll be all right. Don't you want to get out of the rain?"

"I can't think in that dark, crowded place," Emma said. "And today I need to compose myself. Somehow I mind leaving home now even more than the morning I said goodbye to Mother." Her eyes glistened with unshed tears. "When we crossed the river at noon, I knew we'd never turn back. Until today, I kept hoping something would change your uncle's mind. But even the cholera won't stop him. He has gold fever. It's the worst disease of all."

Abby shrugged. She didn't dare admit that when Pa left a year ago, she'd begged him to take her along. Maybe she had a touch of the "fever" herself.

"Abby, I *can't* get back in the wagon yet," Emma whispered. "There's no privacy here. What are we to do? Not a tree or a bush in sight. And everywhere you look, there's a man. Where should a woman go, when the need arises?"

Abby understood, though no one ever spoke plainly about these private things. She looked out across the wet grass, trampled beneath the steady weight of turning wheels and heavy hoofs. Men, wagons, and animals covered the greening swells of prairie in every direction.

"Come on," she said. "We'll find a place and hide behind our skirts."

They walked away from the wagons in the sluicing rain. When they came to a small hummock, Emma crouched in the grass while Abby spread her skirt in a wide semicircle, making a shield of calico to hide her aunt from the jeering eyes of the men.

"Not much shelter, is it?" Emma laughed while Abby took her turn.

Walking back, Abby wondered how Emma managed to look beautiful, even in the rain. "She's got Yankee refinement," Mother had said when they first met her. Emma wore sleek, fashionable skirts that swished and twitched just above the mud. Delicate, hand-knit mitts covered the palms of her hands, leaving her fingers free for cooking and sewing. Will told Abby privately that Emma was too delicate for this trip, but Abby wasn't sure.

Angry shouts interrupted her thoughts. "It came with your hired hand, Parker." She recognized Mr. Grey's rasping voice, and she followed Aunt Emma toward the small crowd of men, huddled near the grave diggers. A dark form, shrouded in sacking, lay beside the shallow hole.

"We never had a speck of illness until he came along. He's bad luck."

Uncle Joseph heaved a wet clod of earth from the ground and straightened up. "Bad luck?" he asked. His voice was cold. "Matthew Reed's all right. He's perfectly healthy. Cholera's everywhere. Look!" He was shouting now, trying to raise his voice above the tumult. "They're all running away from it!"

He pointed to the steady stream of wagons, their drivers and passengers ignoring the dead body and the makeshift grave as they rumbled past.

"I'm lucky to have Matthew Reed," Uncle Joseph continued. "He's a good worker. Besides, I don't mind telling you it was a kindness to take him on. His father died recently. Matthew's all alone in the world."

"And how did his father die?" sneered Mr. Jones,

Herbert Grey's traveling companion. "Did you ask him that?"

There was a great deal of angry muttering, and Mr. Grey shouted, "Look! Here he comes now, on the run. We'll see what he's got to say for himself."

Matthew came up to them, out of breath and streaked with mud. He looked at the hostile crowd with raised eyebrows. "Need help?" he asked.

"We're just trying to clear up a misunderstanding," Uncle Joseph said quietly. "Some of the men thought you'd brought cholera into our company."

Matthew tugged at the pockets of his jacket and pants until each one was inside out. Then he looked in his hat. "Don't see any cholera here," he said.

"It's no joking matter!" Mr. Grey shouted. "Maybe *you* don't have it. But Parker here tells us your father just died. Was it cholera that killed him? They say it's carried on the clothes. I'll bet that's his jacket you're wearing, from the way it hangs on you."

The color drained from Matthew's face until his eyes and cheeks seemed bleached. Abby was ashamed of the way she'd questioned him earlier.

"My father died on board ship," Matthew said at last. "He was in a fight, and it killed him. I don't think I've brought trouble to this company. I'm grateful you were willing to take me on."

"If you're so grateful, why don't you stick around when there's work to be done?" Mr. Jones demanded.

Abby felt uncomfortable. Mr. Jones was right.

Matthew often disappeared at the noon stop, or in the evenings. Where did he go?

Matthew didn't answer, and the circle of men seemed to grow tighter, enclosing him in an angry silence. Suddenly, Captain Foster appeared, holding a shovel caked with mud. "If no one's man enough to dig the grave, you might consider that we'll want to eat before long," he said. "There are fires to build, and the oxen are hungry. We're not going any farther tonight. We owe Mr. Colt the decency of saying a few words over his grave. Now leave the boy alone. He knows more about death than the rest of you."

Some of the men looked ashamed, and the crowd broke up. As they drifted away, Uncle Joseph took Matthew aside. His gestures were angry, almost fierce. What was he saying? Abby wondered.

Emma tugged at Abby's sleeve. "Come on," she said. "Leave them be. We're both soaked through. Let's change our clothes. And Abby, thank you for letting me talk to you. I hope we can become friends on this trip." She squeezed Abby's hand.

Abby went back to her mother's wagon, where she climbed up over the slippery wheel, nearly losing her balance on the rim. Mother lay still on the mattress, her blue eyes staring at the curved hoops above them.

"Mother," Abby whispered. "Are you sick too?"

"No. Just tired. There was nothing I could do for that poor man. Nothing." She closed her eyes.

Abby stared. Mother's face, usually so impassive, looked broken. Would this trip change everyone—even her mother? Mary Parker's tiny frame, stretched out on the pallet, seemed drained of the strength that had held the family together for the twelve long months since Pa had left. Abby pulled off her wet dress and changed into a dry one while rain drummed on the canvas, drowning her thoughts.

May 10. At the Kansas River Ferry.

Dearest Caroline,
It's been a terrible day. A boy drowned when his father tried to float their wagon across the river. The man was too impatient to wait in line for the ferryboats. Instead, he made his oxen swim, pulling the wagon. The current was too much for them—they floundered out in the middle, and the river sucked everything down in an instant. The boy screamed, the oxen bawled, and then they disappeared. I can't get those dreadful sounds out of my head.

The boy's father nearly drowned himself, trying to rescue his son. He was only fourteen, just my age. Why would anyone be so foolish? Emma says, "Gold Fever makes a man crazed." Will Pa be that way when we find him—crazy over gold?

There are other things I don't understand. Matthew Reed, for instance. Whenever we meet a new group of people, he disappears, as if he's looking for someone. And he reads every message beside the trail. (People scrawl things on pieces of scrap wood and leave them for their friends who are traveling behind.) I read them sometimes, when I'm bored, but I never find anything interesting. But Matthew even studies the names on the gravestones. It's awful how many people have died, and the journey's just begun.

I'm wondering about Emma, too. She won't eat, but Mother says she's not sick. When I ask her what's wrong, she tells me there are things I've no right to know. That makes me mad. I hate secrets.

It's finally stopped raining, and we were quite cheerful until the boy drowned. This afternoon, Mother and I boiled a kettle of muddy river water, scrubbed our clothes, and spread them to dry in the sunshine. The shirts looked like birds, resting on the prairie grass. How I longed to jump on Timothy's back! The prairie is so wide, you could gallop forever without reaching the edge.

The line is long; we won't have a place on the boats until tomorrow. I'll write again when we've made it across the river.

Love from your affectionate sister,
Abigail

May 15. Approaching the Vermilion River.

Abby walked beside the wagons, placing one foot before the other in a steady, unbroken rhythm. Ordinarily, she loved these fresh mornings when the sun and wind swept the prairie clean. But today she was angry at Mother. She ignored the hawks soaring overhead and didn't notice the grass greening beyond the muddy track. Small things bothered her: the chafe of her skirts against her legs, the rub of one tight boot on her big toe, the steady thump of Pa's watch on her chest.

She had promised herself she would walk until Mother let her drive the oxen, and now she was afraid she might have to make the whole trip on foot. She didn't understand why Mother was so firm. "It's no job for a young girl," her mother had said. "These are big animals."

It seemed unfair. One day, Mother told her she was a young woman. The next, she claimed Abby was too small. Mother drives, she thought, and she's not much bigger than I am. In fact, she looks like a bird, poised for flight, when she's up on the wagon seat. How would *she* control the oxen if they bolted? Could she stop them with the same sharp tone of voice she used on her family?

Abby wanted a friend, someone like her sister to ease the sense of isolation in the midst of the crowded caravan. But everyone was busy today, leaving Abby to walk alone, gathering wood for the fire. Wagons stretched without a break from one horizon to another, like a sash pulled tight around the earth's waist.

"Get along there! Hup!" Abby was relieved to hear a familiar voice and turned to see the supply wagon roll toward her. Will swayed on the seat with the rocking of the wheels, holding the heavy whip in one hand and the reins in the other. He made it look so easy—it couldn't be much harder than driving their horses at home.

"Will!" she called. "Pull up! These sticks are heavy."

"Whoa!" Will shouted. The animals slowed a little; Abby handed him the bundle of branches and swung herself onto the step below the seat. The oxen lurched forward, and she caught her skirt on the rim of the wheel, tearing it just above the ankle.

"Thank you!" Abby dropped down on the seat next to her brother. He nodded but kept his eyes on the animals. Abby studied him. In just a few months, his whole shape had changed, until he resembled Pa: sturdy and muscular, with their father's short, stubby fingers. His eyes were like Mother's: an intense blue that was almost green. Abby laughed.

"What's funny?" Will asked, giving her a quick glance and then turning his eyes back to the trail.

"I was thinking you have Pa's body and Mother's head. I have Pa's hair and eyes, but I'm like Mother from the neck down."

Will snorted. The oxen stumbled, and he barked at them. Showing off, Abby thought; they're so placid and ponderous they couldn't go anywhere.

"Is it noon yet?" Will asked. "I'm hungry."

Abby pulled out Pa's watch, enjoying the smooth action of the latch as she flipped the case open.

"Only ten-thirty," she said. "You're *always* hungry."

Will shrugged, and Abby thought how Mother goaded him when he loaded his plate a second and third time. "This food has to last awhile," she'd say. "Go shoot something if you're starving."

The wheels hit a bump. "Rough road, isn't it?" Will asked. "Captain Foster says this is the easy part of the trip. I wonder what the mountains will be like."

Abby pulled at the reins. "Let me try for a minute."

Will pushed her hands away. "Don't, Abigail. You know Mother won't let you."

"So what? You're here with me. Besides, if I learned to drive, you could hunt with Matthew. I know how to manage animals. Remember, Pa let me drive the horses, when we were haying. Please, just for a minute. I'll be careful."

"What makes you think Matthew wants a hunting companion? He's off on some private search most of the time."

So Will doesn't know his secret either, Abby thought. Aloud, she begged, "*Please*, Will?"

Will looked around, to see if anyone was watching them, and shrugged. "All right—but just over the easy places. If anyone comes, I take over."

Abby took the heavy reins. They felt limp. When she'd driven Pa's team, in Ohio, she'd always felt a living connection coursing through the reins from each horse's mouth into her hands. But the oxen had no bits and could be driven without the leather traces, if a man wanted to walk beside them. Abby knew she couldn't crack the whip—not yet, anyway. Still, they moved ahead, and she guessed they might keep going whether she sat there or not.

She talked to their wide backs in the same steady voice she used riding Timothy. "Go on, now; easy there. That's right." One of the rear oxen flicked an ear, but the others plodded on, straining a little under the load.

Abby tried to look relaxed, as though this came easily to her. She turned to Will. "Do you stand watch tonight?"

"Yes—look out!" One of the oxen stumbled over a pothole, but the wagon churned forward. When the animals held their pace again, Will asked, "Why do you ask?"

"I'd like to take your turn. Listen for Indians and wild animals. I'd love to be out on the prairie, in the dark."

"You can't do that," Will said. "Driving the oxen's one thing. But the night watch—that's nothing for a girl to do."

"Why not?"

Will's blue eyes darkened with scorn. "You're not serious, Abigail?"

Abby wanted to push him off the wagon. If it weren't such a long way to the ground, if he weren't so strong now, she would have been tempted.

"Of course I'm serious," she said. "What's wrong with it?"

"It's too dangerous. What if a storm comes up and spooks the cattle? What if Indians raid the camp? It's no job for a *woman*," he said, spitting out the last word like a bitter stomach powder.

"It's no job for someone who can't *see* either," Abby retorted. Will looked stung and opened his eyes wide, trying to hide his constant squint. Abby wished she could swallow her words. She knew he couldn't help it if his eyesight was bad. But what had happened to her brother since Pa had left? Had he forgotten all their games? She thought of how they used to hide in the woods, how they'd look for signs of a bear in the thick brambles where the raspberries grew. The first one to stumble on the bear's scat would yell, saying the bear was right behind them—even if the manure was days old.

"Hey!" Will shouted, snatching the reins away from her. "We almost hit that rock!"

Abby rubbed her hands; the rough tug of leather made her palms sore. "You never used to treat me like this," she said. "When Pa left, he told you to take care of us, not to boss us around." She fingered Pa's watch for reassurance and stared at Will's profile. Red spots appeared at the top of his cheekbones, just as they did on Mother's face when she was angry.

"You're not much older than I am," Abby went on, "but you treat me like a child. You only call me a 'woman' because it makes you seem like a 'man.' We're both children on the way to being grown up, that's all."

Will looked embarrassed, and Abby could almost see his old self slip back inside him, as though he kept it hidden somewhere and could put it on when no one watched.

"I'm sorry, Abigail. But surely"—he turned to her, his face red and uncomfortable—"you are *almost* a woman. All the men notice, especially Matthew. Besides, it's not much fun out there in the dark. Sometimes I'm afraid," he admitted.

Abby stopped listening. What did he mean, "especially Matthew"? She couldn't bear to think of men looking at her that way.

"You can have your night watch," she said. "I'll find a way to see the prairie on my own."

Abby jumped down from the wagon, lost her balance, and fell to her knees. Her bonnet flew off her head; the rolling wheels caught the ribbons and churned over the wire and cloth. Good, thought Abby, despite the humiliation of falling. That wretched bonnet always made her feel as though she saw the world through a narrow band. It was just one more thing to confine her, to keep her in the cage made up of skirts, aprons, and "ladylike" manners.

The bonnet lay in the mud, crushed to a pulp. She left it there and took the pins from her hair, tossing her head until the dark red tangles fell onto her shoulders. I'm still a girl, she told herself. A girl wears her hair down, doesn't care if her face is burned and freckled.

I'll never have Emma's pure complexion anyway. I'll just be myself, muddy and rumpled.

She heard shouts rise above the rumble of wheels. Animals slowed and men ran to the edge of the caravan, pointing north. Abby saw a band of horsemen in the distance. They were Indians—a large group, riding slowly, ignoring the travelers to their south. For one long moment, Abby imagined she rode with them, that she could sit on one of those stately horses with poise and grace. She would dress in leggings, soft deerskin pants that allowed her to grip a pony's round sides as he coiled and sprang from a walk to a gallop. He would stretch his neck out flat, until Abby, the ground, the pony, and the wind were fused as one.

The Indians disappeared over a swell in the prairie. Abby ran to Mother and Uncle Joseph, who stood watching next to the supply wagon.

"Mother! Uncle Joseph! Who were those Indians? Where are they going?"

Mary Parker turned and pursed her lips. "Listen to you, Abigail—screaming your lungs out! And no sunbonnet—your dress is torn—"

"Uncle Joseph," Abby interrupted, ignoring her mother. "Will they bother us? Is that why we've stopped?"

He shook his head. "No. They keep their distance here. They're afraid of cholera. We have to be more careful, farther west." He gave her a disdainful look. "Your mother's right. You're a mess. This stop is for bathing—you'd better throw yourself in the river."

Abby let out a whoop. A swim!

"Abigail—please," Mother said. "I know it sounds wonderful—but Joseph, all these strangers. It's not very private."

"You women will swim first, then the men. I'll stand guard."

"Thank you!" Abby said. She could have hugged her uncle, but she knew he wouldn't like it. "Uncle Joseph —what's the name of the river?"

"The Vermilion." He pointed to a spot where the prairie fell away. "Emma's waiting for you there. Go on, before I change my mind. Go ahead."

Abby ran all the way to the top of the steep bank and grabbed her aunt from behind. "Emma!" she crowed. "Isn't it wonderful?"

Emma jumped, then laughed. "You surprised me, Abigail. Yes, it's a beautiful river."

Far below, they saw a clear, rushing stream, sprinkled with stones. *This* was a river for her collection, Abby decided. The Vermilion—she wouldn't forget that name, or the way the water sparkled in the middle and tugged the bushes growing at the shoreline.

"Come on," Abby said, grabbing Emma's hand. "Let's go!"

They slid down the bank like ponies eager for water, laughing as their boots slipped in the soft gravel. Mary Parker followed them into the cool shadows of the cottonwoods that cloaked the riverbank.

"Mother, hurry!" Abby cried. "Please unbutton me." While her mother poked at the long line of buttons,

Abby watched Emma go upstream to undress alone. Why was she so modest? Though Abby couldn't see her, she could imagine how Emma would fold her apron, then her dress and stockings, smoothing out the creases. Abby tugged at her own dirty dress, letting it fall in a jumble onto the wet gravel.

Abby remembered the watch. She lifted it from her neck, slipped it into the deep pocket of her dress, and stood for a minute in her chemise. It was pointless to ask if she could take that off, too. Mother would never allow it.

She strode into the river up to her knees. The water was icy cold, but she plunged in. She lay on her back and kicked with the current until she was out in the middle, gasping as her hands and feet grew numb. Then she turned on her stomach and swam down-stream.

"Abby!" Mother's voice came from a great distance.

Abby stood up, surprised by how far she had drifted, and turned around. It was hard work going back; she had to plow through the current. Abby slipped and stumbled on the rocks. Shivering and laughing, she scooped up handfuls of water to watch rainbows sparkle in the droplets.

Abby was tempted to splash her mother, but she was stopped by the expression on her face. Mother was star-ing at Abby's chest in a way that made her feel naked, exposed.

"Mother—what's wrong?"

"I didn't realize you were such a young woman."

Abby looked down at her dripping chemise. The thin material clung to her body, outlining every curve.

For the second time today, someone had called her a woman. Had she changed overnight? "Don't say that, Mother, please. I'm *not* all grown up, not yet."

"Of course not. But you have a woman's body. I hadn't noticed. You've changed so this year, your father will hardly know you."

How could Pa not know his own daughter? "Pa won't forget me!" Abby protested fiercely. "Don't say that!"

She stamped her foot and closed her eyes tight, trying to see Pa. She pictured the curly red hair and the hazel eyes, like her own, but she couldn't put them in a face. There was no memory of a forehead, a nose or mouth, just the rusty tangle of beard covering his chin. Was this what happened to Pa when he tried to picture his family? Tears streamed down her face, and she waited for Mother's request to "school herself in." She was surprised when her mother spoke in soothing, gentle tones.

"Abigail," she said. "Don't fret. I only meant you've grown. Of course your father will know you."

Abby stumbled against her mother's chest, letting her tears fall. Mother laughed quietly. "How could he ever forget you?" she asked. "There's no one else like Abigail."

Abby stepped back and smiled at her mother through tears. "Do you think so?"

"Of course." Mother sounded more like herself again. "Now get dressed."

Abby felt self-conscious as she squeezed water out of her chemise and pulled on her dress. "Mother," she asked suddenly. "Where *is* Pa? Do you think he's waiting for us?"

"Of course."

Abby stole a look at Mother's face. Two red spots pulsed and flickered beneath her eyes. Abby felt sick. If Mother was worried, that made it worse.

"Why do you ask?" Mother demanded.

"I don't see why he'd write once—and never send another letter. Maybe he doesn't think we're coming. Maybe he's gone home by sea...or something." She couldn't finish the thought; nothing could be worse than to mention death out loud, as though saying the word could make it happen.

"Your pa would never send for us if he didn't plan to be there. And the mail takes months to come by boat— you know that."

Abby was not convinced. Behind Mother's tone, which said, "No more questions", she heard doubt. She scrambled up the steep bank, and stood at the crest of the hill a minute, wringing out her wet hair. If only Caroline were here, she thought. She might answer my questions.

"Have a nice swim?"

Abby whirled around. Matthew stood behind her, his gray eyes resting lightly on her face.

"I suppose you've been watching?" Abby snapped.

Matthew shook his head. "I was tempted. But I had my back turned."

Abby pushed past him, feeling heat rush up into her neck. She didn't believe him, any more than she believed her mother. If this is the summer I had to grow up, she thought, then I wish I'd stayed at home.

May 21. A Sunday near the Blue River.

Abby sat bolt upright in bed, panting. She shuddered and gazed upward at the butter-colored canvas, waiting for her heart to calm down. She had dreamed she was running through a cemetery, trying to dodge the tilted gravestones looming overhead. She stumbled and fell at the foot of the tallest marker, and there was her mother's name, throbbing in the stone.

Abby shivered. She was afraid to look down at Mother's place in bed. Her mother had been sick with dysentery, too weak to do more than moan softly when she needed to leave the wagon. Abby had dosed her with rhubarb and opium, and ignored Will's constant complaints about her cooking. "Your biscuits are like rocks!" he exclaimed one morning, whacking one hard against the Dutch oven until it rang. But Abby was too worried to care, too angry with the men for refusing to stop the wagon train so Mother could find a private spot to rest.

Now Abby lowered her eyes. The straw tick held the imprint of Mother's body, but the bed was empty. Abby jumped up and opened the canvas cover.

Mother stood over a small fire, stirring something in the Dutch oven as though she'd never been sick. Abby plunged back into the wagon and rummaged in the dark corners until she found her clothes. She dressed quickly, and felt beneath the pillow for her knife and watch.

Seven o'clock—she'd overslept. "Mother!" she called, stepping from the wagon out onto the wheel. "You're better!" She jumped down, ran to the fire, and peered into her mother's face.

Mother smiled. "I believe I am. In fact, I'm even hungry, though I hardly dare eat."

"Why did you let me sleep? Shouldn't I help you? Are we leaving late today?"

"One thing at a time, dear girl. It's the Sabbath, and we voted not to travel. All but Mr. Jones and Mr. Grey, of course. I let you sleep because you've worked hard the last few days. We all need to rest."

Mary Parker gave her daughter a long, steady stare. "Go brush your hair," she said. "You're a sight. And fetch some water when you've milked Suzy. We have dishes to wash."

Abby laughed and kissed her mother hard on both cheeks. "Mother's well!" she laughed to herself. She grabbed the bucket and ran, ignoring its haphazard bang against her legs. "She's well enough to scold me!" Abby couldn't remember when she'd ever enjoyed a scolding. She wanted to dance on the green prairie, stretched tight as a bedsheet over the earth.

Abby flung her arms wide and laughed. When Mother was sick, the family seemed shattered, missing her quiet direction. Even Uncle Joseph had moved in a dark, restless silence. Now they could relax. Abby tilted her face back to swallow up the sun, when she heard the clump of heavy boots behind her. Will ran past, carrying two bridles.

"Will, stop! Where are you going?" Abby cried.

Will waved toward the prairie, where pairs of men jumped onto horses and galloped off in four directions. "Matthew and Frank Watson had the last watch," he called over his shoulder. "But Matthew disappeared, and Frank fell asleep. Suzy's missing, and some oxen, too."

Abby bit her lip. Not Suzy! She hurried after Will. "Where did Matthew go?" she cried.

"How should I know?" Will said. "He's done for, this time. Uncle Joseph's fishing. I'll take his horse and start searching. Chester's fast." He stood still a moment, squinting. "You see him?"

"Out there, to the south," Abby said, pointing to some stray horses. "Here, I'll take Timothy's bridle."

"Right," Will said, looping the bridle over her arm. "Find someone to ride the pony. Send them after me—I'll go into the hollows." He whistled for Chester and held out a handful of oats. The big roan trotted toward them and blew his nose gently over the grain before snuffling it down.

"Give me some oats for the pony," Abby said.

Will poured the oval grains into her palm. Then he

slipped the bridle over Chester's ears, jammed the bit into his mouth, and hauled him to a rock.

"Will, don't be so rough," Abby complained, but Will jumped from the rock onto Chester's back and kicked him to a startled gallop without looking back.

Abby whistled to Timothy. The pony cantered to her and nuzzled his head against her chest. "Here, boy," she said, cupping her palms beneath his lips. The delicate hair on his nostrils tickled her fingers; when he finished chewing, she slipped the bit into his mouth.

"Come on, boy, over here," Abby cajoled. As Timothy followed her to the rock, she heard Pa's voice in her head: "If you can't get on the horse yourself, you don't deserve to ride." How many times had Pa watched her swing up onto the pony's slippery back, only to slide down, just missing the crest of his withers? She was tall enough now to do it on the first try.

Abby pulled up her skirts until her bare knees rubbed Timothy's barreled stomach. She kicked the pony to a canter.

"Go on, Timothy," she urged. "We know where Suzy would go, don't we? Some place cool and wet."

The pony's ears twitched back and forth as he cantered easily over the hard ground. Abby crowed with delight. How long since she'd felt his rough spine beneath her? She wove her fingers through his coarse mane. "I won't leave you so long next time, I promise," she said. "We're going to ride together a lot now." Timothy flicked an ear backward, as if he approved.

The prairie changed underfoot. They left the beaten,

grazed area and rode into taller grass. The wind stirred the wildflowers and the beaded heads of grasses, making the earth rise and fall like a featherbed, shaken and gently settling.

The prairie rolled and curled into mounds where a few trees grew. Could there be water there? Abby looked behind her. The wagons were sinking below the horizon. She'd better take her bearings. She glanced at the sun, then flicked open her watch. She was riding due north; she'd have to return with the sun on her left. Pa would be proud of her now.

Timothy snorted. Abby kicked him back to a trot and scanned the prairie for movement. Though she'd never seen the ocean, Abby imagined its infinite swells must resemble this rolling sea of grass.

They rode for a long time. Abby was lost in thought when Timothy snorted and halted suddenly. He pawed the ground, his skin rippling with fear. Abby felt her own hair prickle at the nape of her neck. "What's wrong?" she whispered.

She listened. The wind's song broke into three notes: a low, mournful sound, a steady hiss, and above it, a high-pitched jangle.

"That's Suzy's bell, isn't it? And I hear oxen bawling. Come on, Timothy!" She kicked his sides. The pony danced beneath her, trotting another hundred yards to the spot where the prairie fell away. Abby had learned that these sudden drops often meant water, and she wasn't surprised when they pulled up above a small stream. Suzy and two oxen stood in the shallows, switching their tails through swarms of mosquitoes. Abby slapped the insects on her hands and wrists, and slid off Timothy's back.

The deep grooved tracks of oxen were imprinted in the mud at her feet. Close beside them, four enormous pawprints splayed and gathered in the dark muck. Timothy stiffened.

"Easy, now," said Abby, scratching his ears. "That's why you were so nervous. It's a bobcat, isn't it? Let's hope he's gone home, now the sun is up."

Suzy mooed, long and low. "Come on, boss, let's go home. Time for milking. Come on up, bossy." Abby spoke in the lilting, singsong voice she always used for the cow. Suzy climbed the bank, her bell swinging with every ponderous step. When she crested the bank, she stared at Abby with her almond eyes.

Abby laughed. "Where have you been, girl? And look at your bag, swollen with milk. Come on, I'll help you."

Abby squeezed a few jets of milk onto the ground, then squirted some into her mouth. She swished it around before she swallowed it; the milk was warm and sweet. She felt like a barn cat, crouched beside the cow's flank, her mouth wide open to catch the hot liquid.

She stood up and looked at the oxen. She had to bring them back, too. Abby pulled Pa's knife from her pocket, snapped open the smooth blade, and cut a long willow switch from a trailing branch.

"Come on up, boys," she called. To her surprise, the oxen bawled, followed Suzy's trail up the bank, and stood quietly in front of Abby, as though waiting for their next set of instructions.

Abby laughed. "Hold on," she said, and clambered up on Timothy's back. "Now, gee up!" she shouted, nosing Timothy behind them while she tapped their rumps lightly with the switch. They lumbered off in a ragged line, following Suzy south toward the wagons.

Abby took one quick look behind her at the stream. She didn't know its name, but that didn't matter. It would go in her diary as "Suzy's Creek."

"Whoa!" Abby called. The oxen stopped obediently. "Walk on," she said, and they moved forward, trusting her voice.

One by one, the covers of the wagons rose up on the curve of the horizon. As she neared the campground, Abby saw two riders wheel and gallop in her direction, one tall and thin, the other short and stocky. Matthew and Will. Abby sat up straight on Timothy's back.

Will was shouting before he reached her. "Abby— you weren't supposed to ride Timothy! Where did you find them?"

"In a little hollow by a stream," Abby said. "I knew where Suzy would go. And these two lummoxes were with her." Abby pointed at Matthew, who drew up beside them. "You let them go. Where were you?"

Matthew sat quietly on the horse and took off his hat. "I can't really explain it to you," he said lamely. "Give me time. I'm sorry about the animals. I didn't know Frank would fall asleep. I'm sure grateful, Abby. We found everything but these three. I didn't know you were so good with horses."

Abby ignored the compliment. "You can't just leave whenever you feel like it and expect us to understand forever."

"I know," Matthew said. "I'm sorry. It's a family problem I have to settle. That's all I can tell you."

Abby met her brother's eyes. *What now?* Will shrugged, and they rode back to the wagons in silence, the cattle running eagerly ahead of them.

"Get ready, both of you," Will said as they caught sight of their uncle's tall figure striding to meet them.

"I'm not afraid," said Abby, giving Timothy a kick. "Uncle Joseph can say what he likes." She trotted on ahead and called out, "Ho! Uncle Joseph! Look what I found!"

Uncle Joseph scowled up at her, his hands on his hips. "Abigail Parker—get off that horse. What do you mean by running off and not telling your mother? She's sick enough as it is."

Abby tossed her head, gripped the pony's sides, and grinned down at her uncle. "She's not sick this morning. Besides, I found Suzy—*and* the oxen."

Uncle Joseph's eyes grew dark, and he clenched his fists. "You've got an answer for everything, haven't you?" he asked. "What will your mother say when she hears you're riding like an Indian, with your legs on both sides of the horse? Now get down, before I pull you off."

Abby yanked at Timothy's mouth. The pony side-stepped beyond her uncle's reach. "Mother knows how I ride," Abby retorted. "Anyway, *Pa* taught me. *Your* brother."

"Abby." Will sounded shocked, but Abby didn't look at him. She kept Timothy moving in an awkward dance, away from her uncle's lunging body. Suddenly, Matthew rode between them, almost knocking Uncle Joseph to the ground. He jumped from his horse and faced her uncle with his hat in his hands.

"Mr. Parker," Matthew said. "I must apologize for all the problems. It's completely my fault."

"I should say so," Uncle Joseph snapped. "The first Sabbath we have to rest—and you disturb it with your foolishness. If the stock were gone, you'd owe us more than an apology. Right now, I'll thank you to stay out of my affairs with my niece. She needs a whipping, not a white knight to rescue her."

Abby's face burned, but she kept her eyes fixed on Matthew, afraid of what he might do. Even with his hat off, he was taller than Uncle Joseph, and there was something calm, almost dignified, about the way he stared at her uncle.

"Uncle Joseph, don't be angry," Will said quickly. "I told Abby to catch Timothy. Let's give Matthew another chance. After all, how could he know Frank Watson would fall asleep? Frank's to blame as well."

Abby held her breath. It wasn't like Will to protect her. And why should he stand up for Matthew now?

The horses stamped uneasily in the silence. Finally,

Uncle Joseph threw up his hands in exasperation. "Abigail and William, you're both your father's children—
too sassy and stubborn for your own good." He turned
on Matthew. "I accept the apology on one condition:
that it never happens again. If so, you're out of this
company—forever."

Before anyone answered, he was gone, driving the
two oxen before him with long, angry strides and harsh
commands.

When his voice died away, Matthew looked up at
Abby. "Well, that's over," he said lightly.

Abby stared at him. "Maybe it is for *you!*" she
snapped. "I'll be tied to the wagon for days now." She
kicked Timothy's sides. "Come on, boy," she said. "Let's
take care of that cow."

Abby rode off, feeling Matthew's hurt stare burn
through the back of her dress. She didn't care. After all,
hadn't she befriended him from the beginning? All he
did was hide things and get her in trouble.

When she had milked Suzy and tethered the pony,
Abby went to find Will. He was pounding Chester's
stake into the ground with furious strokes; his eyes
danced with anger, and his lips were pulled into a tight
line.

"Will," Abby said. "Thank you for standing up for me.
Why did you do that? And why help Matthew?"

"I don't like the way Uncle Joseph talks to you," Will
said in a gruff voice. He straightened up and set the
hammer on the ground. "And don't you see? Matthew
will have to tell us now. If we protect him, he'll have to

share his secret, won't he?"

Abby looked across the campground. Matthew was tethering horses, rubbing them down, and whistling. She couldn't hear the tune, but his movements were relaxed and careless, as though the morning had barely touched him.

"I don't know," she said. "Somehow I think it won't be that easy."

May 25. Beyond the Little Blue River.

The sun broke suddenly through a hole in the thick cloud cover, sending low-slung shafts of light into Abby's face. She covered her eyes with a dusty hand and yanked at the straps of her borrowed sunbonnet, sweeping it up onto her head. In spite of the wide, curved brim narrowing her view of the prairie, the sun still sought out her hazel eyes, making her squint.

Wasn't it time to stop for the night? Abby dragged her feet and waited for the captain to signal the final halt of the day, but the continuous rumble of wagons and human complaints went on without interruption.

"Abigail!"

She turned to see Matthew riding high on the supply wagon. Whenever he smiled like that, she had to grin back—even though she had tried to keep her distance this last week.

"Hop on with me," Matthew called. "The oxen can handle it."

Ordinarily, Abby would rather ride Timothy or walk than suffer the jolts in the wagon. But Uncle Joseph wouldn't let her touch Timothy until Sunday when they were resting. Right now, her legs ached from long hours on the trail. Besides, there was always the chance Matthew might tell her his secret.

"Thank you," she said. "I'd be grateful for the ride."

The wagon slowed, and Abby gathered her skirts in her right hand, ready to climb up. Before she knew it, Matthew grabbed her left arm, hoisting her onto the seat beside him. She landed off balance, and almost fell backward into the wagon bed before Matthew caught her by the shoulders. Her bonnet slipped off, and her loose coil of hair tumbled from its pins. Abby righted herself and laughed.

"That was quick work," Matthew said. "I didn't want to stop the oxen."

Abby stretched the kinks out of her legs and looked down. Her boot laces were untied, and the hem of her dress was caked with mud. Sparks from their campfire had sprinkled holes over the stained calico. I look like a salt shaker, Abby thought. Shake me, and my dirty petticoat comes through.

"Honestly," she laughed. "I'm falling to pieces."

Matthew nodded. His gray eyes scanned her face and

clothes until Abby felt embarrassed. "It suits you," he said.

Abby's face burned. Did he mean to tease her, or was that a compliment? She tried to find something interesting to watch in the caravan ahead and was surprised to notice two wagons coming toward them.

"Matthew, look," she said. "People going east. I wonder what went wrong?"

A disheveled group of travelers walked beside their tired animals. Abby checked quickly, as she always did, looking for Pa. But these people were older than her father. The first man limped next to his dusty oxen, while the second man's head sagged, drooping toward the ground like his mule's. Then she noticed the woman; she was tall and bony with an arrogant, almost triumphant face. Unlike her companions, she walked with quick, energetic steps.

"Looks like they've 'seen the elephant,'" Matthew said. When Abby looked puzzled, he asked, "Know where that expression comes from?"

Abby shook her head. "Tell me."

"A farmer went to town," said Matthew, "hoping to see the elephant at the circus. He had a wagon loaded with chickens and eggs to sell. Soon the circus parade came by with its enormous elephant. The farmer was delighted, but his horses were terrified. They spooked, overturned the wagon, and dumped eggs and chickens all over the road. 'Who cares?' said the farmer, when he saw the mess. 'I've seen the elephant.'" Matthew nodded toward the defeated travelers. "I guess these folks saw what's ahead, and that was enough," he explained. "Wonder if that could happen to any of us."

"I hope not," Abby said. "Otherwise, we'll never find Pa, or the person you're looking for."

She glanced quickly at Matthew, to see how he might respond, but he was silent. She would have to approach him differently. He'd been stubborn so long, she wondered if he'd ever start talking.

"I noticed you studied those people pretty carefully," she said casually. "Did you wonder who they were?"

Matthew's eyes twinkled. "I believe you're trying to get something from me. Actually, I was looking at the woman. She looked so happy—did you notice?"

"Yes," Abby said. "As if she couldn't wait to go home. I guess a lot of women feel that way. Emma, for instance. She begged Uncle Joseph to stay in Ohio."

"How about you?" Matthew asked. "Is that how you feel?"

"No," Abby said. "I wished Pa would take me last year, but he refused. Now—I don't know. I thought it would be different, traveling. I didn't realize I'd have the same old jobs on the trail as at home."

Matthew laughed. "Did you think we wouldn't have to work?"

"I don't mind working—I just don't like 'womanly' jobs, as Mother calls them. It doesn't matter where I am, I'd rather work with animals or cut hay than cook and scrub." Abby stopped herself. "I don't mean to complain. Really, I like traveling. Being in a different spot every night; finding new rivers and creeks for my collection—"

"Your 'collection'?" Matthew interrupted.

Flecks of light danced in his eyes, and Abby couldn't tell if it was laughter or sunlight. Why had she said that? She wanted to pry a secret from Matthew, but all she did was give away her own.

"It's nothing, really—I'm just keeping track of the rivers and streams we cross."

"That's a good idea. Do you write them down?"

Abby glanced at him again. He seemed genuinely interested, not teasing this time. "Yes," she said. "I put them in a diary. Someday, when there are maps of all this, I'll be able to see where we've been. I can remember the leeches from last night, or the clams in the Big Blue, or swimming in the Vermilion."

"Why are you so eager for California?" Matthew asked. "Is it your pa?"

"That's part of it," Abby said. She looked up, where masses of dark clouds coiled and piled toward the heavens. A hawk swept across the gray backdrop, soaring and floating on wind currents to sail effortlessly higher.

"Don't tell me *you* have gold-rush fever," Matthew said.

Abby hesitated. She found herself wanting to talk to him, in spite of his teasing. "See that bird?" she said. They watched it dip its wing, plummet toward the prairie, and then swoop upward again, like a tiny boat riding waves of air.

"I dream about being free as that hawk," Abby said. "When I'm with my family, I feel like a magpie dropped in a bluebird's nest. I think it will be different in California. I could be—" Abby caught herself, too shy to finish the thought: that she could be herself, for the very first time. Abby glanced at Matthew, to see if he would laugh at her, but his expression had changed completely. He looked puzzled, almost sad.

"How would it be different?" he asked at last.

"In Ohio, they printed letters from men who went to California," Abby said. "One man talked about how few women there were, and how they were so independent. He said one ran a boardinghouse; another cooked meals for people in her tent. Women out there are gold miners and bankers; they keep piles of gold dust under their beds." Abby stopped and pursed her lips tight. She had almost told him what else she had learned, reading the paper; that some women had made their own claims, bought their own land. She might share some of her dreams, but that one was sacred.

"So you're out to break some rules?" Matthew asked.

"I guess so," Abby answered.

Matthew laughed. "Abby, you're doing that already. And you're right—your family doesn't like it. What would your father say?"

Abby straightened her back. "Pa *likes* me this way," she said fiercely.

"I bet he does," Matthew said. "I do, too."

A tense knot of excitement formed in the pit of Abby's stomach. She couldn't look at Matthew, but she felt him inch closer on the seat.

"One more question," Matthew added. "Do you mind?"

Abby tossed her head. "Only if you promise to answer one of mine."

"That's fair," Matthew agreed. "All right. Let's talk about another girl, someone a little older than you."

Abby nodded, puzzled. Was this another game?

"Say she longs for something in her life. She's not as clear in her mind as you are; she doesn't know yet exactly what she wants."

Do I? Abby wondered. She glanced shyly at Matthew, but he kept his eyes on the trail.

"All right," he said. "Say the girl's ready to leave home, but her parents decide she should marry. They even pick out a husband for her, a settled, older man who needs a wife. But she hates him. What should she do?"

"That's easy," Abby said quickly. "Run away, of course."

"I was afraid you'd say that," Matthew said.

"Why?" Abby asked. "That's what *I'd* do."

Matthew nodded. He was serious now. "I'm sure you would. But would you go alone? You'd manage, of course, though you might be lonely; you enjoy people."

Abby couldn't believe the way Matthew made such casual references to her personality, as if he'd known her forever. She stared at him, but he didn't notice. "What about this girl?" he asked. "Would she be all right on her own? Or would she feel better going off with someone else—a man, perhaps?"

Abby was annoyed. "How can I answer that?" she demanded. "I don't even know her."

"True," Matthew said. The wagon lurched suddenly. Abby slid along the seat and felt Matthew's firm waist against her own, the hard angle of his shoulder. She surprised herself by leaning against him for a minute.

"Hello," Matthew said, grinning down at her.

Abby sat up straight. Even though she felt hot all over, she liked the sense of his long legs beside her, the closeness of his hands resting lightly on his knees. She prayed silently for the wagons to keep moving steadily west forever.

"Why are you so interested in what I think?" Abby asked, suddenly feeling bold. "Most men aren't."

"They will be," said Matthew dryly. "Is that the question I have to answer?"

"No!" Abby said quickly, remembering the reason she'd climbed into the wagon in the first place.

"I'm teasing," Matthew said. "The truth is, you remind me of my sister. I miss her, that's all, and when I talk to you, it makes me feel at home."

Abby knew she was about to untie the knot of mystery entwining him. She thought of a skein of yarn lying in a tangle on the floor. If you picked it up in just the right way and found the end, the whole mess of knots would fall away and you could wind it rhythmically into a smooth ball. Matthew had just presented her with the piece she needed.

"Here's your question," said Abby. "Are you looking for your sister? Did she run away?"

Matthew didn't answer at first, but a shadow crossed his face, and Abby knew she was right. "Go on," she said. "Tell me. You promised."

"You won't tell Will—or your uncle?"

Abby shook her head. Matthew looked like a little boy, for a moment. He was so tall, everyone treated him like a man. Right now, he seemed younger than her brother.

"No one," she said.

There were shouts ahead, and the wagons began to pull out of the trail to form the circle for the night. Matthew grabbed her arm, holding it tight.

"You're right," he said. "It *is* my sister." He lowered his voice until Abby could barely hear him. "She ran away from home with a gold miner. None of us liked him. I'm not sure she did either, though she told me she loved him." Matthew paused, his voice tight with embarrassment. "They weren't even married. It's shameful, to think of my sister living with a man that way. Now you see why I've kept it a secret."

Abby nodded, but she stayed quiet, looking down into her lap.

"It broke Mother's heart," Matthew continued. "Dad and I promised we'd bring her home. Cover it up, if we could, let her start fresh. But of course, Dad's gone now. I'm on my own."

"Matthew," Abby said, wincing. "You're pinching my arm."

"I'm sorry," he said and released his grip. "Abby, do you think I'm doing the right thing?"

"I don't know," she answered honestly. Thoughts tumbled about in her head. She knew she could never be so brave, although she'd boasted about running away. She'd never felt that way about a man either. In Ohio, her friends might whisper their secret feelings about boys, but they'd never declare them openly, much less act on them so brazenly. But perhaps Matthew's sister thought the conventional way of doing things was silly. Or perhaps she was desperate. Abby could imagine how she would feel if her parents forced her to marry someone she didn't like.

"Matthew, what if she wants to be with this man?" she asked suddenly. "Do you think you have the right to stop her? What if she won't come home?"

"I don't know. But I have to find her. I just can't believe it's what she really wanted to do. She always leaps into things, without thinking. And it's not just what other people might think. Abby, I'm afraid of the man. He's no good. Besides, I promised my father I wouldn't give up the search."

Matthew jumped from the wagon, and Abby followed. He had said more now than in all the weeks since they'd met. She couldn't believe his dark, layered secret was finally out in the open. "Matthew, what's her name?" she asked softly, aware of people nearby.

"Molly," he whispered. "Molly Reed." He unbuttoned his shirt pocket, pulled out a leather case, and opened it. "Here's a daguerreotype."

Abby took the picture in her hand and tipped it until the image, printed on glass, swam into focus. A small, wiry girl with black hair grinned up at her. She wore a faded calico dress, and her hair hung loose to the elbow, with a flower caught behind one ear. She looked carefree and proud.

"She's pretty," Abby said. "How old is she?"

"Only sixteen. Much too young to be married. If she *is* married," Matthew added.

"Matthew, lots of girls get married at sixteen. Anyway, that story you told me—I assume that was Molly."

Matthew nodded.

"It sounds as though your parents were ready for her to be married. They just wanted to choose the husband."

"You're right," Matthew admitted. "Abby, I'm sorry I was so secretive. It's just—I didn't know how you'd feel about what she's done."

"I don't care about that," Abby said quickly, and she meant it, even though she knew her own family might be shocked. Who could know what went through this girl's mind when she ran away? Abby studied the miniature again and glanced at Matthew. "She looks like you," she said. "Especially her eyes."

Matthew folded the leather case and put it back in his pocket. As he took the heavy yokes from the oxen, he whispered, "Now you know why I go away so often. And why I check every wagon train, even the ones coming east. There's always the chance they'd give up and come home."

"I do the same thing," Abby admitted. "Looking for Pa."

Matthew seemed surprised. "Really? You think he'd give up on mining? I thought he sent for you."

"He did," Abby said. "But we've had only one letter. No news since this winter." Abby took a deep breath. "That's why I painted the sign on the wagon. I knew Pa would see it, if he's headed east. I didn't want him to miss us. But now the sign's fading, in all the rain."

Matthew laughed. "Abigail," he said. "I doubt anyone could miss your family. I wouldn't worry. But I'll help you keep watch, if *you* help me. We can work together. What does he look like?"

Abby thought a moment. "His hair is redder than mine," she said, "and curlier. He has a full beard. He's short and stocky, like Will. He has a loud voice and a deep laugh. People like him for that. He gets angry quickly, and then it goes away. Mother says I have his temper." She caught her breath. Tears formed in her eyes, and she had to turn away.

Matthew touched her shoulder lightly. "We'll find him," he said firmly. He stiffened and stared out over the endless, rolling prairie. "We'll find them all," he said. "And when I get hold of Judson Hall—"

"That's the man Molly ran away with?" Abby asked.

"That's right."

"I wouldn't want to be Mr. Hall when you find him," Abby said. She frowned. "I don't imagine Will would

run after me if I left home. You must really care about
your sister."

"I do," Matthew said. "And I think you're wrong
about Will. Abby, you're not thinking of flying away, are
you?"

Abby laughed. "Not now. Even though I feel like it
sometimes."

"That's a relief," Matthew said. "I wouldn't want to
chase after two of you."

Even without a mirror, Abby knew her freckles had
deepened in color as the blush spread from her neck to
her cheeks. When she saw Mother coming toward
them, she felt relieved. "You'd chase me, would you?"
she mocked. "I'm pretty fast on a horse, you know." She
waved at Mother and whispered quickly, "Don't worry.
I won't say anything."

All evening, Abby plunged into her chores with a
burst of energy. She hauled more water than they
needed, staggered under armloads of cottonwood
branches, and volunteered to clean and fry the fish Will
caught, ignoring the clinging smoke as she stood over
the campfire. She avoided Matthew; the stolen secret
rattled and thumped inside until she thought her rib
cage might burst from the pressure. She didn't feel safe
until she was in the wagon at last, perched on the
lumpy mattress in a spot where she could just see
Matthew.

Firelight moved in liquid shadows over Matthew's
face and glistened on the canvas wagon cover. He was
playing the harmonica; a sad, haunting melody that

made Abby hold her breath. Was he calling for his family, scattered all over the earth? For the first time, she realized how lonely and lost he must feel inside. Maybe he joked and teased to cover the sadness.

Matthew looked up and caught her eyes. In an instant, the melody changed; as it surged into a major key, Abby shivered with pleasure. The song spoke of their search, and how they would share it together. She sang along with the thin, reedy notes:

> *Oh, Susannah, don't you cry for me,*
> *I'm bound for California*
> *With a washtub on my knee.*

Mother began to sing from the back of the wagon. Emma and Uncle Joseph joined in from beyond the fire, and Abby smiled. Matthew had united her family with his song, pulling their voices together in the dark. Soon, Abby thought, our family will be complete again. It has to be. We'll find Pa—and Molly Reed, too.

She sang louder, perched on the edge of the wagon, beaming at Matthew. Men from other campfires joined in; their voices running up and down with the notes, until the black bowl of sky filled with song. She imagined the tune, caught in skeins of clouds, flying up to join her distant hawk, who would carry it gently away into the darkness.

May 29, 1850.

Dearest Caroline,
Your letter was waiting for us when we arrived at Fort
Kearney. Mother and I read it again and again. We
could almost imagine you sitting on the big oak stump
outside your cabin, with the baby crawling in the dust
at your feet. I wish you were here with me!

There are no stumps on the prairie, just a few trees
near the river. I'm sitting on the wagon tongue with my
feet on Mother's trunk. You wouldn't believe what peo-
ple throw away: stoves, shovels, bedding, crowbars,
bake ovens, barrels, harness, bacon. They dump every-
thing on the ground until we can hardly walk from one
wagon to the next. Mother and Uncle Joseph argued all
day long about what to leave behind.

Will shot an antelope today! It was such a beautiful
creature, with red-brown fur, a thick shaggy mane, and
branching antlers. He brought it back draped over
Chester's back, and the poor thing stared at me with
dead eyes.

You'll never guess how he killed it. Captain Foster
told him antelope are curious about bright colors. So
Will took Mother's red shawl, hung it over his
shoulders, and sat very still on the prairie, near a herd
of antelope. This one came close, to see the shawl—and
he shot it. Isn't that cruel? I thought I'd never speak to
him again, but then I tasted the meat and had to admit
it was delicious.

Will was so proud to shoot something. Of course, it's only because he lured it so close and could see it clearly. He swaggered around the fire at dinner, pointing an imaginary gun. It seemed very childish to me.

Matthew told me why he disappears so often, but I've promised to keep it a secret—even from you. He's been nice to me; it's good to have a friend so far from home.

Two soldiers at the fort have offered to take letters east for us. Day after tomorrow, we leave to follow the Platte River. I was disappointed there was no news from Pa. Maybe we'll hear something at Fort Laramie. This letter comes with love from

your affectionate sister,
Abigail

May 30. Fort Kearney, on the Platte River.

The noon sun was hot; someone had pulled up the cover on one side of the wagon to dry the damp bedding. Abby climbed over the seat and jerked the strings to let the canvas fall, enclosing her in rich, honey-colored light. She edged through the tightly crammed rows of trunks and grain bags to the foot of the bed and slipped one hand under the mattress.

"Ouch!" Abby cried as something sharp pricked her fingers. "What's under there?"

She lifted the straw tick and found a cache of Mother's possessions; a bundle of needles, shanks of homespun yarn from their black ewe in Ohio, packets of seeds, and the letters from Pa and Caroline. Abby sucked her bleeding finger and picked up a bunch of twisted roots. Anyone else might have thrown these away, but Abby recognized dried cuttings from the flower garden. She smiled and wondered if Mother's flowers would bloom in California. They knew so little of what life would be like there.

Abby pulled a small collection of her own treasures from the deep pocket of her apron and slipped them under the mattress. In addition to the diary where she kept her list of rivers and streams, she had a pen, some writing paper, and a few worn books. She smoothed the quilt down over everything and stretched out on the bed.

"Pretty lumpy," she giggled, and jumped up, rocking the wagon. She wondered when Mother had hidden her special things—last night, after they cried over Caroline's letter? Abby felt close to her mother for a minute, thinking how they'd chosen the same hiding place, and was tempted to share her discovery. She rolled up the canvas, giving her a view of Mother and Uncle Joseph standing on opposite sides of the campfire. Uncle Joseph's chin stuck straight out, and Mother slapped her spoon angrily up and down in the iron kettle.

Abby slipped out of the wagon and down over the

wheel, crawling stealthily up behind them until she could hear their conversation.

"Be sensible!" Uncle Joseph was shouting. "We can't carry a flock of chickens across the mountains, much less a cow. It's foolishness! This is the *easy* leg of the trip!" His voice softened a little. "They'll never survive the desert, Mary. It's cruel to take them so far. Let's feast on the chickens, and sell Suzy. Captain Foster says we'll need cash for the ferries."

Mother's lips made a straight, narrow line below her flaring nostrils. "I have all the cash I need," she said in a strained voice. "And I notice you relish the eggs we eat now and then. You seem to appreciate the butter that churns itself as the wagon rocks along. Besides, Emma savors the milk—don't you see that? It's the only thing she'll eat."

Uncle Joseph ran his hands through his hair and paced back and forth. "That's something else—I don't like the way you coddle Emma. There's no call for it. She's a grown woman. She doesn't pull her own weight."

Mother stared at him, opened her mouth, and shut it quickly as she caught sight of Abby.

"Abigail! You ought to be ashamed, eavesdropping on us. Have you nothing better to do? Here—take this bucket and bring some clean water. The cornmeal is sticking. Tell Matthew and Will to come for dinner."

Abby ran to the banks of the river and knelt down beside a seep hole. As she dipped her bucket into the stagnant water, she chided herself. If only she'd kept hidden—then she'd know why Mother was worried about Emma. Would Uncle Joseph kill the chickens? That wouldn't be so bad, but what about Suzy? Could she hide her somehow?

"Need help?"

Abby jumped up, sloshing water on her dress. "Matthew! You scared me. What's the matter?"

Matthew's eyes had a strange, distant gleam, reminding her of Pa when he first started talking about gold in the rivers.

"One of the soldiers at the fort recognized Molly," Matthew said. "I showed him the daguerreotype. He remembers seeing her with an earlier party of miners. She was with a man—sounds like Hall." Matthew paused and took a deep breath. "There was only one other woman in their company, an older lady who stood up for Molly and protected her."

Matthew's forehead wrinkled with worry. His hair fell down over his eyes, but he didn't notice; he was staring into the distance, as though he might see his sister wandering toward him over the endless sea of grass.

"You could leave—and chase after her," Abby said.

"Trying to get rid of me?"

"No, I don't want you to leave. I mean—" Abby stumbled over her words. What *did* she mean?

"Don't worry," said Matthew. "I can't go anywhere without a horse. And they say only trappers and mountain men can make this trip alone."

"You could take Timothy," said Abby in a low voice.

They stared at each other in silence for a long moment. Finally Matthew spoke. "You're offering me your pony?"

Abby nodded. She couldn't say anything.

Matthew shook his head in disbelief. "Abby, I couldn't do that. I know how much Timothy means to you. And imagine what your uncle would do! No, there must be another way to catch Molly. We'll think of something."

Abby held her breath. How had she come to this point? Would she always give things away, when Matthew was around? First her private thoughts and dreams, now the pony—was she bewitched? Abby took a step backward, as though everything about him—the smell of his jacket, the way he tossed his hair from his forehead, the easy sound of his laugh—were part of some invisible net he had dropped over her.

"Let's go back," Abby said, trying to hide the trembling in her voice. "Mother's waiting dinner for us."

She returned to the fire, rushing ahead of Matthew's footsteps. Everyone else was eating already; Uncle Joseph sat on a barrel, gnawing on a piece of antelope meat. He scowled at Abby.

"Well, Abigail, I see you *finally* found water. Lucky you had the help of your white knight again."

Abby thought she might burst into tears. Why couldn't he leave her alone?

"Joseph, please." Emma spoke from her rocking chair, where she sat with her hands folded quietly in her lap. "She does her share. Let her have some fun."

Abby sighed gratefully. At least Emma was on her

side. She opened her mouth to say something when Uncle Joseph began to shout at his wife.

"Where were *you* when this meal was prepared?" he demanded, thrusting his chin forward. "And why don't you eat? You'll starve before this trip is over."

No one spoke. Everyone watched Emma's face turn a deathly white, like a new moon beneath the dark coils of hair. Her black eyes grew liquid and large, but she didn't move or speak.

"Well?" Uncle Joseph cried.

Abby shivered. Her uncle's beard was speckled with grease and soot; his scowl was cruel.

"Here you sit," Uncle Joseph said, standing and waving his empty plate in the air. "Comfortable as can be, while Mary waits on you hand and foot and Abigail's off making eyes at young men. Well, I've told Mary there's to be no more coddling. You ought to have better manners. Stand up and give her the chair, and wait on your elders, both of you."

Emma stood up so slowly, Abby thought she might faint. "I'm so sorry, Mary," she said, offering her the rocker. "Forgive me. I never thought—"

Mother waved her hand. "Sit down, Emma. I'm stronger than you are now. You'll feel better before long. Don't trouble yourself."

Uncle Joseph slammed his plate down on the crude planks that made their table. "Mary, don't you see? That's just the pampering I'm talking about." He drew himself to his full height and looked down on his wife.

"Enjoy it tonight, if you must. Tomorrow, the chair stays here."

Emma clutched the rocker's curved back with white knuckles.

"Joseph Parker," she said. "You've torn me away from my family." Her voice quavered, then steadied. "When we first wed, you promised I'd never have to leave my mother. You broke that vow within a month. Well, I have news for you. I'm carrying your *child* on this god-forsaken journey. You're asking me to risk my life, and that of our unborn baby, because of your greed. How dare you deny me the comfort of the one thing I call my own?" Emma took a deep breath. No one moved.

"Leave it behind, if you must," Emma said firmly. "But you'll have to leave me as well."

A baby! Abby was shocked. That explained every-thing: the headaches, the missed meals, the way Emma's dress was always unbuttoned at the waist. Abby's cheeks burned with embarrassment. How could Emma speak about her condition in front of so many men?

A heavy silence hung over their fire and spread to the rest of the campground. Even the animals were still, and there was no wind to rustle the grass. Emma turned her chair around firmly and sat down, crossing her feet at the ankles, as if sitting in church on Sunday morning.

Abby stole a look at her uncle. He stared at his wife's back as though some dreadful snake or insect were crawling there, and his face became crimson, then a deep purple. He lurched toward the chair, raising one hand over his head.

Mother grabbed his arm. "Joseph! Would you hit her? Please, think of the baby!"

Joseph wrenched away, letting his arm fall. "Emma, you should have told me," he began, looking helplessly from his wife to his sister-in-law. "Did you know about this?" he demanded.

Mother shrugged her shoulders. "No one told me," she said. "But I guessed. I've just been through it with Caroline, don't forget. It's wonderful news."

Uncle Joseph opened his mouth and closed it again.

"A little cousin!" Abby cried. "Will—won't that be fine?"

Her brother stared at her, turned on his heel, and disappeared into the bustle of men beyond their campground. Uncle Joseph followed, and Matthew cleared his throat.

"Congratulations, Mrs. Parker," he said, tipping his hat. Then he, too, disappeared.

Emma was crying softly, and Mother leaned over her. "They'll leave us behind," Emma wailed. "I know they will." She looked up into Mother's face, her dark eyes soft with tears. "That Mr. Grey and Mr. Jones—they complain about us all the time. This will be the last straw for them, won't it? No one wants a pregnant woman on this journey. I saw Will's face. And Joseph's. They're afraid the train will abandon us."

"Nonsense," Mother said. "Captain Foster's in charge. He won't leave anyone behind. Now you rest and compose yourself." Her voice became low and soothing; Abby couldn't hear the words. She cleared away the dinner things. She hadn't eaten, but she wasn't hungry now.

When Mother joined her, they scrubbed congealed grease from the plates, washed and dried the cups and other dishes. The rattle of tin seemed magnified in the hollow of their silence.

"Go speak to Emma," Mother whispered finally. "She needs a friend."

Abby crept up to her aunt and touched her shoulder. Emma looked up. Tears streaked her cheeks and ran down onto her lace collar.

"Emma, I'm so glad about the baby!" Abby said.

Emma's lips quivered. "Abby, I made a fool of myself! Here I sit, waiting for Joseph to apologize, or say he's happy about the baby, but how can he? After I spoke in such a shameful way, in front of everyone." She gripped Abby's hands with her long, gloved fingers. "Abby, I'm afraid. Do you think they'll send me home?"

"I don't know," said Abby honestly. "But don't worry. We'll fight for you."

Emma's face seemed to break. Abby stared. Her aunt looked like a frightened little girl. Was she younger than they thought? And if so, how could she stand being married to Uncle Joseph? Why, he was nearly forty!

"Emma, how old are you?" Abby blurted.

"Promise you won't tell?" Emma whispered.

Abby nodded, although she wondered how many secrets she could keep.

"I'm just eighteen," Emma admitted. "Joseph thinks I'm twenty-one. Mother lied to him. She thought he'd be such a good match for me—a settled widower, with his own farm. She never thought he'd take me away."

Emma reached out and took Abby's fingers in one gloved hand. "Abby, you see why I can't feel like your *aunt*—we're almost the same age. More like sisters. I never had a sister," she added. "It was always just Mother and me, after my dad died."

"I'll be your friend," Abby said quickly. She felt she'd betray Caroline if she used the word *sister*.

"Thank you. Abby, I meant it—I'm not leaving this chair unless it goes in the wagon." Emma folded her hands in her lap, leaned back, and closed her eyes.

Emma slept all afternoon, while Abby and Mother repacked the wagon. Uncle Joseph took Matthew hunting, and Will hovered on the edge of the campground, moving sacks of beans and cornmeal from one wagon to another. When the sun began to drop, Mother called out, "Will! Bring me the ax, will you?"

Will reached under the supply wagon and lifted Pa's heavy ax from its hooks. Abby heard a heavy thud, a sharp squawk, then silence. In a moment, Mother appeared holding a beheaded chicken by the feet while its neck and wings thrashed inside a bucket.

"Abby, boil some water," Mother said. "And get ready to pluck them. Will, take the ax, and kill the rest."

"Mother, why—" Abby began, but her mother shook her head.

"No complaints. You heard what your uncle said. Now, do as I say, both of you. When you're done, chop up the cage. It will save us wading across the river to find firewood on the islands."

Will found the ax behind the wagon, pulled another chicken from the cage, and held it down with his foot.

"Wait!" Abby cried. "You'll chop your toes off!"

Will ignored her, raising the ax over his head and letting it fall with a dull thud on the chicken's neck. He turned his head away, and the chicken escaped, staggering across the campground with its severed head dangling.

"Oh, Will—you didn't cut it all!" Abby screamed. She ran after the bird, caught it, and pushed it to the ground. She slashed its neck with her knife, kneeling on the chicken until it stopped its frantic heaving.

Will's face was ashen. "You always were better at killing things," he admitted quietly. "Why don't I pluck, while you chop them up?"

"All right," Abby said. Why were they both whispering? Did they want to hide the ugly murders from Emma? Her back was turned, and only the wind stirred the chair gently. Was she really asleep?

Will and Abby spent the rest of the afternoon killing and plucking the chickens. After a few hours, the birds were splayed out on the wooden table, their skins bruised and prickly with the stubs of feathers. Abby wrinkled her nose as she carried a shovelful of entrails to the latrines. Everything smelled of blood and death. This was the worst day of the trip.

She washed her hands in the river, but the water was so muddy it seemed pointless. She dragged her feet coming back, and was startled to hear Emma's voice.

"Abby! I felt the baby move!" Emma cried when Abby was standing in front of her chair. Emma held one hand on her belly. "A little quiver—your mother calls it quickening."

Abby was speechless. She suddenly realized what this baby meant—that Emma shared a bed with Uncle Joseph in ways she didn't like to imagine. Emma's body would grow swollen, the way Caroline's had, a boast to all the world about what goes on in the dark. Abby blushed. She would *never* do that with a man, never!

Emma stood up and took Abby's hands. "Don't look at me like that," she begged. "Don't be angry. I'm afraid. How can I do this without my mother? There are no doctors here."

"I'm not angry, Emma," Abby said. "It's just . . . a surprise, that's all. And don't worry. Mother knows what to do."

What would it be like, to feel a child move inside your body? Abby didn't want to imagine it. She nearly gasped with relief when she heard Mother's voice behind her.

"Come on, girls. Enough chitchat." Mother's apron was stained with blood, her hair was escaping from its neat coil, and her face was smudged and dirty. "Time to load the chair and cook supper," she said firmly.

Emma raised her eyebrows. "But I thought—is there room?"

"Of course!" Mother laughed. "We brought it this far, didn't we? And now that the chickens are dead, there's plenty of extra space."

"Oh, Mary—you didn't!" Emma cried. "You gave up your chickens for my chair? I feel so selfish."

Mother laughed, a short, dry sound. "Once in a while, Joseph is right," she said, "though none of us wants to admit it. Those chickens wouldn't have lasted much longer. They weren't laying well. I'm sure they'll be tough as leather to eat. Anyway, you'll need your chair, to rock the baby when it's born."

Emma's eyes filled with tears. "Mary, do you think Joseph will ever forgive me? What if he sends me home?"

Mother shook her head. "Don't worry about Joseph. Just wait until nightfall, when no one can hear him. He'll be telling you how happy he is. Right now, he's scared. Most men are. But there's no need. You're young and strong. This will be a California baby, and Abby and I will see to it that it's born safely. I promise."

Mother expects *me* to help? Abby wasn't sure she could. But when she saw the way Emma raised her chin to meet her sister-in-law's determined smile, Abby took a deep breath and threw her arms around her mother. "Now it's your turn to be an aunt!" she cried, squeezing Mother's tiny waist. "I can tell *you* what it's like."

"Why, so you can," Mother said, and for once she allowed Abby to finish the hug, even returning it slightly before she stiffened and pulled away.

"Come on," Mother said. "The men will be here any minute. Let's hoist the chair before they get back."

They carried the rocker stealthily to the wagon—like three thieves, Abby thought. She remembered the hidden belongings under her mattress. That was a secret she shared with her mother—and now the three of them were in partnership together, over the chair and the coming baby. As they lashed the rocker to the wagon with a heavy rope, Abby caught Mother's eye and winked. And she thought maybe—although it was so subtle she couldn't be sure—her mother winked back.

June 11, 1850. Leaving Ash Hollow.

Dearest Caroline,
What a miserable time I've had! Just after Fort Kearney, I came down with dysentery. I lay in the wagon for days, covered with dust and desperate for privacy. Thank goodness for Mother—I knew she'd never leave me beside the road to die, the way some people do when their friends have cholera. We pass graves every day; I just look the other way.

Uncle Joseph blamed my illness on water from the seep holes, and brought me river water to drink. It's the color of coffee, and so thick I could chew it. Until a few days ago, everything made me retch.

Yesterday I was better and walked a little. We came to Ash Hollow, a steep place where we locked the wheels and lowered our wagons with chains and ropes. I was as weak as the oxen, sliding down in the deep sand. At the bottom, we found a real spring, with clean, clear water. Nothing ever tasted so good!

Today I took a bath in the North Platte River. It soothed my mosquito bites, but I couldn't feel clean, swimming in muddy water. The river bottom was strange; I could feel it shift beneath my feet. Another river for my river scrapbook. We will follow it all the way to Fort Laramie.

I'm sitting in Emma's rocker now, looking up at the bluffs. If I could climb to the top, I might see Chimney Rock. We think Pa might have carved his name there last year. I hope to find it!

Did Mother write you? Emma's having a baby! We're keeping it quiet, for fear Mr. Grey or Mr. Jones would push us out if they knew. Uncle Joseph seems pleased, although he doesn't say much about it. Emma's taken it hard; she gets the sick headache often. Mother's little box of medicines and herbs is always open.

It's very crowded here. I know the wilderness is all around us, but we can't see beyond the mass of people. Instead, I close my eyes and dream about the Yuba River. I imagine a rushing stream with gold flecks on the bottom, and Pa standing in the middle.

Hug little Moses for me. I pray you are well.

Your loving sister,
Abigail

June 14. South Fork of the Platte River.

Abby stared at the dark numerals on Pa's watch. "Ten o'clock?" she murmured. "It's so dark."

Matthew nodded. "A storm's coming. Hope we reach Chimney Rock before it hits."

Abby dropped the watch chain around her neck and glanced at Matthew. He sat calmly on the wagon seat beside her, as if the rock meant nothing to him. Had he forgotten their plans to climb it?

For days, Abby had walked long miles beside the oxen. As her strength returned, her impatience mounted. She knew they moved forward; the passing islands in the river convinced her of that. But Chimney Rock was remote. The flat light of the prairie distorted distances, until Abby decided, one morning, they must be rolling over a grassy wheel.

"We'll *never* get there," she'd said to Will a few days ago.

"Where? The rock?" he asked, settling a yoke on two oxen. "Of course we will. But what's the rush? You planning to climb it?"

Abby shrank from him. Had Will overheard her whispered conversations with Matthew? His face always grew dark when Matthew approached. Was he suspicious?

Now Chimney Rock loomed ahead, but dust obscured it, hanging like moving smoke around the wagon train. Abby coughed and pulled a kerchief over her mouth.

"Rain might settle the dust," Matthew said, clearing his throat.

Abby nodded. Clouds massed like smoke, coiling in eerie, yellow-green spirals from the stone chimney. The rock was like a tornado, dropped upside down with the narrow end skyward; the funnel fused to the ground.

"Help!" Abby cried. The wind shifted without warning, wheeling around behind them and sucking dust through the wagon. Abby gasped for breath. "Better stop!"

"No!" Matthew shouted. "Hold them a minute. I'll find oilskins. Tie things down."

The wind tore his words away. He shoved the reins into her hands and disappeared. Abby smelled fear rolling off the oxen's backs.

Rain fell in dense, heavy drops, searing the dust. The oxen snorted and lurched forward; Abby pulled back, straining to keep her seat. She braced her feet against the boards beneath her. Lightning danced in the clouds, and the lead ox bolted, dragging the rest of the team with him.

"Matthew!" Abby screamed. "Come help me!"

The heavy weight of an oilcloth dropped onto her shoulders. Matthew's knees dug into her back as he put an arm on each side of her and gripped the reins just below her closed fists.

"Hold tight!" he shouted. "They're going to run!"

The wind was roaring, and the sound intensified.
Abby heard the clatter of stones on metal and felt something cold sting her cheeks and forehead. She winced,
ducking her chin. Hailstones bounced from the wheels
of the wagon and rolled off the backs of the oxen into
the ruts. Lightning flashed and crackled again, and the
oxen began to run before the wind, maddened by the
pain of falling stones. They tossed their heads and
stumbled out of the trail, dragging the wagon over the
prairie as though it were weightless.

Abby gasped. Hail burned the tops of her ears and
seemed to widen the part in her hair. What if she were
thrown from the wagon? Would the wheels crush her
body as easily as they had smashed her bonnet weeks
before? Only the firm press of Matthew's legs against
her back offered any safety. The hail grew bigger, but
Abby sucked in her screams, determined not to cry out
in front of Matthew.

"Want to get under cover?" he called.

Abby shook her head and hunched her shoulders,
shivering beneath the cold, pelting stones. "No!" she
screamed.

Matthew let go of the reins with one hand and
dropped his hat on her head. Before she could protest,
he had folded her hands beneath his own until they
held the slippery reins together.

Abby bit her lip, keeping her eyes riveted on the
oxen. One glance at the desperate, heaving blur of the
prairie and she could imagine the wagon exploding,
splintered like dry twigs while she and Matthew flew in

tiny fragments over the rough ground. Every bounce of
the wagon brought the taste of her breakfast—flapjacks
and bacon—into her throat.

Abby's legs shook as she strained to keep her seat.
They hurtled past an overturned wagon, then swerved
to avoid a mule, lying with legs askew. Would Suzy end
up that way, dragged and strangled behind her wagon?
Abby shuddered and closed her eyes, wishing it would
all disappear. It seemed hours before she opened them,
and they were still careening over the ground. The hail
changed suddenly to a driving, soaking rain.

The oxen slowed their pace, as if finally accepting
that there was no shelter anywhere. Little groups of
frightened horses huddled together, rain streaming
from their backs. Men ran toward them from different
directions. One held a cooking pot overturned on his
head; another man's shirt hung in shreds from his reddened shoulders.

Matthew whistled in disbelief. The wagon shuddered
to a halt; the oxen stood trembling, while steamy breath
rose from their flaring nostrils.

Abby and Matthew were completely still for a moment, oblivious to the rain pouring off the wagon cover
onto their shoulders. At last, Matthew took a deep
breath and dropped the reins.

"Quite a ride you took me on!" he said, and jumped
down.

Abby couldn't move or respond. She watched
Matthew kneel beside the oxen, checking their legs for
bruises. She still felt his knees in the small of her back.

And something was wrong with her hands.

Abby uncurled her frozen fingers from the reins. Dark, bleeding stains crisscrossed her hands, spreading from purple welts at the base of her thumbs.

"Abby!" Matthew called. "Look where the oxen took us!"

Abby blinked away tears, trying to focus. The red, sloping base of Chimney Rock rose before them, set in a pool of bunch grass and hailstones. Before she could climb it, she *had* to cool her hands somehow. She stood up, still in a daze, and jumped, holding her hands high above her head. In a moment, she was down on the ground, plucking balls of ice from the grass and rubbing them across her sores.

Matthew stared. "Abby, what are you doing?"

"I burned my hands," Abby muttered. She picked desperately at the ground, frantic for the cool touch of ice on her skin.

"Burned—how?" Matthew reached for her hands, but Abby snatched them away.

"Don't touch them!" she cried.

Matthew whistled softly. "I won't hurt you. Just let me look."

Abby balanced on her knees and opened her hands, showing him the red sores.

"No *wonder* we kept hold of the oxen," Matthew said. "Here, sit still a minute."

He grabbed a pail from the wagon and searched the tall grass for hailstones. Abby opened her bleeding palms to the rain, which was falling gently now. In a few minutes, Matthew returned with a thick layer of ice in the bottom of the pail. Abby took two handfuls and held them tight in her fists. Don't cry, she told herself. Whatever you do, don't cry.

Matthew set the bucket under the wagon. "Ice water for lunch," he said. "And the wagon's in good shape— one wheel's a little loose, and there's a big hole in the canvas; nothing we can't repair. We were lucky."

Abby couldn't look at him. His tone was quiet, so full of sympathy she knew she'd weep if he said another kind word. She took a deep breath to steady her voice before she spoke.

"Should we look for the others?" she whispered.

Matthew shook his head. "We can't go anywhere, not now. The oxen are worn out. This was our noon stop, anyway. I'll tether the animals and go on up the rock, while you rest."

Abby scrambled to her feet, forgetting her pain. "Wait a *minute*," she protested. "We planned this together, remember? If I don't climb the rock, neither do you."

Matthew laughed. "Excuse me, ma'am," he said with a mocking bow. He straightened up quickly. "I forgot, for a minute, what sort of girl you are."

Abby bristled and her face grew hot. "What do you mean—what 'sort of girl I am'? You'd better think about what sort of person *you* are."

Abby knew her neck and face must be covered with angry splotches, but there was nothing she could do about it. "You can't keep me from going," she said. "If you don't like the sort of girl I am, never mind. I'll find Pa's name on my own, and we can forget about your silly sister." Abby stomped off in the direction of the rock, her wet skirts dragging at her heels.

"Abby, wait a minute!" Matthew called. He ran up in front of her and took her by the shoulders.

Abby twisted away. How could he smile at her like that? She couldn't bear it.

"I need my hat back," he said quietly, and snatched it from her head. Abby felt her hair tumble down onto her shoulders.

"I like it when your hair's down," he said. "And I like *you*, you ought to know that." He laughed. "Now that I know what your pa's temper is like, I'm a little nervous about meeting him."

"Well, don't worry!" Abby cried, ignoring the tears that streamed down her face. "You'll never have to meet Pa. You'll be gone with your sister as soon as you find her."

Matthew threw his hat to the ground. "How do you know?" he demanded, and brushed the hair off his forehead with a quick, nervous sweep of his hand. "What makes you so sure I'll find Molly? She may be dead, for all I know."

He turned on his heel and climbed into the wagon, disappearing beneath the torn cover. Abby sat still in the grass, shocked by the despair in his voice. How many times, since she'd met Matthew, had she said the wrong thing? He always seemed so light-hearted, it was

easy to forget he *was* sensitive beneath the surface—
particularly about his sister. Did he really think Molly
had died? Abby wiped her face and stood up, letting
her bruised hands dangle by her sides.

In a few minutes, Matthew reappeared, carrying
stakes, a tin of salve, and a pair of gloves.

"Matthew," Abby said softly. "I'm sorry."

"You're going to need gloves to climb that rock,"
Matthew said, as if nothing had happened. He didn't
look her in the eye but kept his eyes focused on her
hands as he pulled a clean handkerchief from his
pocket. "Open up, please," he said, touching her
clenched fingers.

Abby obeyed, and held her hands open, allowing him
to dry her palms and rub salve into the sores.

"Am I hurting you?" he asked.

Abby shook her head, but tears rolled down her
cheeks again. She felt pain and wasn't sure which hurt
more—her hands or her pride.

When Matthew finished, she met his eyes and was
relieved to see his slow, steady stare return, masking
laughter. They stood still for a moment until Abby realized he still held her hands lightly in his own. She
blushed and snatched them away.

"Thank you," she said. "Let's go, before the others
come." She felt her anger melt and an unfamiliar shy-
ness settle in the pit of her stomach.

Abby pulled the gloves carefully over the burns while
Matthew unhitched the oxen and tethered them. They

lowered their heads and sank to the ground.

"Poor things," Abby said, grateful for anything else to talk about.

"They'll be all right," Matthew said. "They can rest here. Come on, before your uncle puts us to work." He looked down at her and smiled. "Neither one of us knows how to be calm about our families, do we?" he asked. "Let's go see if our two runaways left their mark on this strange piece of stone."

June 14. On Chimney Rock.

Abby and Matthew climbed the southeastern slope of Chimney Rock in silence, saving their breath for the steep scramble up the ridge.

"Matthew!" Abby called. He stepped easily over the rocks above her, as though the hailstones and the runaway wagon had never happened, as though he could walk this way—one careful step after the other, higher and higher—for days.

"Matthew, wait!"

He stopped and rocked slowly from his heels to his toes. Abby came up beside him, panting, and drew a deep breath. "Matthew, do you think—could Molly climb the chimney? How high could she go?"

Matthew craned his neck to look at the peak, which seemed to part the clouds with a sharp finger. "Too high, I'm afraid," he said. "At least to the top of this ridge, if she had time." He turned and gave Abby a quick, shy smile. "Afraid we might have to scale it?"

Abby nodded. "Knowing Pa, I guess we might. He wasn't afraid of heights. When we built our house, he'd run around on the ridgepole. Mother could never make him come down. He was like a kid, taunting us to catch him."

It was a relief to talk to Matthew this way. Abby felt they had left their bad feelings on the prairie with the milling animals. But then she thought of Pa's face, peering down at her from the great height of their roof, and a deeper sadness settled over her. She'd never see his name on this rock. Why hadn't she known that before? Of course he'd climb higher than she could ever go—he was fearless. But she couldn't turn back now.

As they climbed higher, Abby tried to pick out individual names from the blur of letters that marked the trail in every direction. Initials, whole names, and fragments were chiseled and gouged into the sandstone. Worn by wind, rain, and the passage of feet, the letters made a ghostly record of each person who'd scaled the rock. Abby's eyes veered from the stony trail to the shifting letters and back again, until she was nearly dizzy with the effort.

They were both breathing hard now, but when Matthew turned to offer Abby a hand, she shook her head and pulled herself up, hoisting her skirts to a height Mother would find unladylike. If she couldn't find Pa's name, she promised herself, at least she could tell him she'd struggled up the hill on her own.

Abby smiled. One minute she imagined she'd never find her father, and the next she dreamed of conversations they'd have together. She wondered if the same blind hope kept Matthew cheerful when he knew they might never find his sister. Maybe he couldn't stand it otherwise, with his father dead.

Abby forced herself to hum a wordless tune, swallowing the dark, darting worries while they climbed another hundred feet up the ridge. The rock dried to a dull clay-red as the sun appeared. When they finally reached the base of the chimney and stood panting beneath the sheer cliff, Abby knew she'd reached her limit. Her body felt like a pincushion, stabbed at every joint with aches from the wild ride and the stiff climb.

"I'm going to rest, just for a minute," she said, and sank against the smooth stone, letting her spine ride down the rock until she sat with her legs out in front of her. She waited for her breathing to slow and watched the small groups of people who were starting to climb the base of the hill.

"We'll have company soon," Matthew said. "I think I'll look around here while I can. If I find anything, I'll call you."

"Will you climb higher?" Abby asked.

He shook his head. "Not without help. Anyway, I don't think Molly would go up there."

"But Pa would," Abby whispered. "And I can't."

Matthew craned his neck to look at the chimney, then let his eyes rest softly on Abby's face. "He wouldn't expect you to climb that, would he?"

"No." Abby turned away, holding back tears.

"Don't give up yet. We may find them," Matthew said. "Sit here a minute. I'll be right back." He touched her shoulder so gently she thought she'd imagined it, then disappeared along the ledge.

Abby nestled against the hot stone. Her dress began to dry, and she drifted into a half sleep. Soon, an image of her father wove through her thoughts, intermingled with Matthew's grin. The two faces shuttled back and forth in a dream, until a shadow crossed her face, waking her with a start.

A stocky figure blocked the sun. For one heartbreaking moment, the gleam of Pa's belt buckle, his short, stocky legs and his toed-in boots teased her. Had he found her at last? But it was Will, wearing Pa's clothes as he had since his sixteenth birthday. Abby scrambled to her feet and rubbed her eyes.

"Will! You surprised me! Where did you come from?"

Will pushed his hat back from his forehead. "I could ask you the same thing. What are you doing up here?"

"Matthew and I—" Abby hesitated. Weeks ago, they'd been determined to uncover Matthew's secret together. Now she was part of the mystery, but Will was left out. "We wanted to carve our names on the rock," she said, and then added quickly. "How did you get away from Uncle Joseph?"

"I said I had to rescue you. But I lied."

Something quickened in Will's face. It was more than the rare threat of rebellion against their uncle. An intense desire blazed in his eyes, as though something outside himself had pushed him up the cliff. Abby suddenly felt blind, as though she hadn't noticed her brother since they left Ohio.

"You want to find Pa's name too," she said.

"Of course," Will answered. "And I will. I've planned it since Fort Kearney."

So that was the reason for his moodiness! "*I* planned it too," Abby said. "But I didn't know it would be like this." She pointed to the spire above them. "You'll have to climb it for me. Will you?"

Before Will could answer, they heard Matthew shout, "Will! Are you all right? Was anyone hurt?"

Abby was ashamed to think she'd forgotten her family. Especially Emma—the storm must have been torture for her.

"Everyone's fine," Will said quickly as Matthew joined them on the narrow shelf. "Just shaken. A wheel came loose." He paused. "Well, Matthew, feel like climbing higher? I want to find Pa's name."

Matthew grinned. "You're both determined, aren't you? Well, I'm game." He gave Abby a long, piercing stare. "That is, if Abby keeps looking down here. I haven't found anything yet."

"Will and I are sure Pa would go higher," Abby said.

"Right," Matthew said. "But you never know."

Will turned to study the rock, looking for carved toeholds, and Matthew leaned close to Abby. "See if you find any ladies' names up here. You might be the only girl that's climbed this high."

Abby understood. If Matthew left to find Pa's name, she'd have to look for Molly's. She tossed back her hair. "There won't be any ladies where you're going," she said mockingly. "We're too smart to climb a cliff." She winked at Matthew, to show him she understood. "Go on," she continued. "Uncle Joseph will be after us soon."

Will and Matthew began to climb the rock, helping each other from one narrow foothold to the next. Abby was suddenly afraid. "Will!" she cried. "Pa never asked us to find his name! He never mentioned Chimney Rock. Maybe he didn't stop here."

"He never mentioned any place except Yuba River!" Will called back. "We don't even know where he is now. Too bad. I'm going up."

He wonders if Pa's alive too, Abby realized. "Good luck!" she called, and turned away. It was better not to watch.

She inched along the chimney's thick base, angling her feet into the hill. She understood Will's bitterness and recognized the sense of abandonment in his voice. She'd felt it herself. Too bad they couldn't talk about it. She began to sing, to put it out of her mind.

> *You calculate on sixty days*
> *to take you over the plains . . .*

Names circled the rock and danced up and down before her eyes. Was everyone a John or a Thomas? There were no women anywhere; Matthew was right. Abby was proud to be the first girl up this high; she sang a little louder.

> But there you lack for bread and meat,
> for coffee and for brains . . .

Abby reached a huge boulder, edged around it, and stopped. The wall of the chimney dropped to the prairie, and the shelf disappeared. She would have to turn around.

Her hands throbbed. She pulled off her gloves, one at a time, and dabbed her oozing palms with her apron. Should she go back to Will and Matthew? She craned her neck to see them, but the blank face of the chimney seemed to glower and move toward her through the clouds.

> Your sixty days are a hundred or more,
> Your grub you've got to divide . . .

Abby stopped singing and held her breath. Two bold names shimmered in the sunlight.

Molly Reed, said the first; the crude, straggling letters running downhill to meet *J. Hall, 1850*.

"I found her," Abby whispered. "Matthew, here she is." And then, remembering she was alone on the narrow ledge, Abby fumbled in her pocket for her knife. The carving looked new. Was Molly traveling just ahead?

Her hand trembled as she gouged at the rock. She scratched an *A*, two *B*'s, then a *Y* into the sandstone.

The knife rubbed and deepened the sores on her palms, but she didn't care. *She* had found the name. She hummed again, finishing the song as she cut *Parker* into the sandstone.

> *Your steers and mules are alkalied,*
> *So foot it, you cannot ride.*

She remembered her accusation this morning. If they did find Molly, would Matthew leave them? Abby stared at the rock, trying to sort her thoughts. How could she wish for Matthew to stay, when he'd made her so angry? Should she keep this discovery to herself?

"Don't be silly," Abby said out loud, carving again. Finding Molly's name in the rock wouldn't lead them right to her. Besides, she'd be furious if Matthew saw Pa's name, but kept it to himself.

Abby stood back to admire her carving, then slipped the knife into her pocket. She dropped the gloves on the ground to mark the spot, then crept back along the ledge, wishing she could call down to the distant wagons, fluttering toward each other on the prairie. She longed to shout at Matthew, invisible somewhere above her.

"Aaabby!"

Will's voice came from a great, hollow distance. Abby scrambled to the next outcropping and looked up. Matthew and Will clung to the rock, one above the other, like leeches on a giant's leg.

"Hallo!" she called, waving. "Down here! Did you find something?"

"Yes! It's Pa!" Will gestured wildly, lost his footing, and fell. Abby stumbled toward him as Matthew's hand jutted out and caught Will by the elbow. For a terrible, endless moment, Will dangled helplessly overhead. Matthew's body wavered and shook.

"Let go!" Will groaned. "You'll kill both of us."

Abby stood helplessly beneath her brother, trying to reach his flailing legs. Suddenly, one boot caught an outcropping of rock. Matthew grunted, his face contorted, and flung Will against the stone. Her brother clutched the air and then met solid rock with his free hand.

"I've got it," Will cried hoarsely. "Let go, for God's sake."

Matthew released his hold and Will slid down the rock, like a child coming down a pole. He toppled close to the edge of the cliff. Abby caught his collar and heaved him away from the abyss. Will slumped against her and collapsed, knocking her down.

Abby lay stunned for a moment, then pulled herself up. What had happened to Matthew? She looked around wildly, half expecting another body to hurtle toward her. But Matthew was inching his way backward down the rock, from toehold to toehold, his chunky boots settling carefully against each tiny outcropping.

Abby stared at Will. His face was white and still; his left arm splayed out at a strange angle.

"He's fainted," Matthew said, coming toward her. He moved slowly, as if his feet were detached from his body. He bent and touched his fingers to Will's wrist.

"He's got a fine pulse," Matthew said. "He'll come around."

In the back of her mind, Abby heard prayers, as though someone else were pleading, just behind her skull, for her brother's survival. Please, the voice begged in a whisper. Let him be all right. I promise I'll read the Bible, pay attention to Uncle Joseph on Sundays.

Will's eyelids fluttered and opened. He groaned. "What happened?"

"You tried to pull me off the rock," Matthew said. His voice sounded strained, and his hands trembled as he fumbled with Will's collar to unbutton it.

Will flinched. "Don't touch my arm," he whispered.

"I'll be careful," Matthew said, peeling the shirt back until the left shoulder appeared, pasty-white next to a ring of tan at the collar line. Will bit his lip.

"The shoulder's crooked," said Abby.

"Pulled from the socket," Matthew agreed. He winked at Will. "Guess I jerked your elbow a little too hard. You flew by me awful fast. No bullwhip for you, for a few days."

Will blinked at Matthew and his eyes widened. "You saved my life," he said. "How did you catch me?"

"I don't know," Matthew admitted. "It was luck." He slipped his hands beneath Will's good shoulder, hoisting him to a sitting position. "Think you can make it down the ridge?"

Will slumped against Matthew's chest. "I don't know," he whispered. They were all quiet for a moment, and then Will turned to Abby. "Pa was there, all right," he said, and closed his eyes.

How would they get him down? Abby stood up, brushed herself off, and untied her apron. Using her knife, she tore at the stitches, ripping the sash away from the material until she had a long, narrow band of fabric.

"Prop him up," she said. She wrapped the cloth around her brother's neck, under his forearm, and back up to his neck again to form a sling. Then she tore two more strips from the apron and bound her own palms with the dirty fabric. When Matthew and Will were silent, she said, "I never did like aprons, anyway."

Matthew laughed. "A doctor in our midst," he teased. "Thanks."

"What happened to your hands?" Will asked.

"She ran a race against everyone on the prairie," Matthew said. "And won."

"You drove through the storm?" Will stared at Abby in disbelief.

"We both did," Abby said.

"I couldn't hold the oxen back without her help," said Matthew.

"Not really—" Abby began, but Will interrupted.

"You were right to learn," he said. "You'll get all the driving you want now. I won't be able to do anything."

"You'll be all right," Abby said, although she was worried. She didn't like the way his arm was twisted like a rope, or the way his face had crumpled. And what about Molly's carved name? Could she and Matthew leave Will alone?

"Let me rest here a minute," Will said, pulling away from Matthew to lie on his side. "Then I can walk. Uncle Joseph may come after us." He sighed and was quiet.

Abby waited until her brother was breathing steadily, and then touched Matthew's sleeve. "I have to show you something," she said. "I found an easier way down. Will you take a look?"

"Sure." Matthew followed her along the rock until they reached the stretch of ledge where the trail narrowed. "Abby, wait," he said. "This is impossible. We can't bring Will this way."

"I know. Just come a little farther." She stopped, and glanced at him over her shoulder. Her gloves lay just ahead on the ground, but she had to know something before she gave her secret away. "Was it really Pa's name, do you think?"

"Yes. It said, 'William Parker, 1849.' Will carved his own name next to it. He got as far as 'W. Parker, J.' before he fell. Now, don't you think we ought to get back?"

They had edged around the last outcropping where Abby had left her gloves. She stopped to pick them up. "Look at the rock," she said, hiding a smile.

Matthew studied the stone. "Abigail Parker —" His jaw fell open and he stood transfixed, staring at the chiseled letters. When he turned around, his eyes shone; Abby was stunned when tears formed on his lashes and spilled onto his grimy cheeks.

"She's alive," he whispered, tracing the letters with

his fingers just as Abby had done. "Molly Reed . . . J. Hall . . ." Matthew frowned. "She's not married yet, is she?"

"Maybe not," said Abby. "Are you glad?"

"I don't know. If she's living like a married woman . . ." Matthew hesitated. "Then she's lost all her self-respect." Matthew turned and gripped Abby by the shoulders, startling her. "Abby, we *have* to find her. The carving looks fresh. Promise you'll help me?"

Abby knew she was blushing from deep in her throat up to her scalp. For a moment, she wondered if he might kiss her, and what she would do if he did. But he let go.

"Of course," Abby said. "I'll go to Will now, while you carve your name. I left you a space." And she scrambled over the rocks without looking back. Everything felt too big for her suddenly: the trip, the storm, the search for lost fathers and sisters—and, most difficult of all, these strange feelings for Matthew, which made her so confused she forgot to thank him for saving Will's life.

Abby scanned the hill and saw a bony, familiar figure toiling up the ridge toward her. "Uncle Joseph! Up here!" Before she knew it she was running and sliding toward him, lurching over the rocks until she careened against his chest.

"Why Abigail, what—"

"Uncle Joseph," Abby gulped, tasting tears. "Will's hurt. He found Pa's name on the chimney. But he fell and twisted his shoulder."

Uncle Joseph gave her an awkward pat and pulled

away, staring down at her. Abby waited for the cloud of anger to darken his eyes, but, to her surprise, he looked up at the hill and laughed.

"Ha! I should have known they'd go up there—father and son both. Watch out, brother William," he called, shaking his fist at the bony peak. "We found you here— we'll find you in California!"

Abby couldn't believe her ears. Uncle Joseph missed Pa? It was too much to understand. She thought of her brother lying in a heap on the rocks and pulled at her uncle's sleeve. "Please come," she begged. "Will needs help. And you won't be angry, will you? He's in pain."

Uncle Joseph tried to frown, but his eyes glittered, reminding Abby of her brother.

"I should be furious with all of you," he said. "But you've caught gold rush fever, like the rest of us. Come on, take me to Will. Lead the way. Show me how you climbed the hill."

June 15, 1850.

Dearest Caroline,
We're camped near Scott's Bluff, a few days from Fort Laramie. Uncle Joseph went to the Trading Post to fix a broken axle. Mother and I are writing to you while our bedding dries in the sun.
I've been on my first buffalo hunt! I was up early

yesterday, looking for Suzy, when I saw clouds of dust in the distance. I ran to Timothy and got his bridle on just as someone shouted, "Buffalo!" I jumped on the pony and followed the crowd of men, keeping a safe distance from Uncle Joseph. I didn't want him to see me.

We chased the buffalo to the foot of the bluffs, where they milled about, trapped. They're huge creatures—I was afraid they might turn on us. "Shoot just above the brisket!" the captain cried. Before long, four were dead on the ground.

The men argued; some wanted to slaughter the whole herd, but Captain Foster said they'd waste their bullets. So they let them go while the captain showed everyone how to butcher the dead ones. I crept close to watch.

This is what they do: first, they heave the poor creature onto its belly and spread out the legs, so it can't fall over. They cut away the skin at the shoulder, where the fur is thick and curly. Then they slice along the spine, through the smooth hair, all the way to the tail. When they peel the skin away, they spread it out on the ground as a "table" for the chunks of meat.

The worst was watching them take hatchets to the shoulder and chop at the ribs. Mr. Grey gouged out the tongue with his knife, while Frank Watson took the liver.

Timothy smelled blood, whinnied, and pawed the ground. That's when Uncle Joseph saw me. I think he'd have taken his belt to me, but I rode away. We almost made friends on Chimney Rock, but I guess I've ruined *it again. How else will I see the prairie dogs pop out of their holes, or watch the antelope running wild? I have to escape sometimes. I can't gather buffalo "chips" all day.*

Buffalo meat tastes delicious, but we use their dung for fuel! We take turns filling burlap sacks with the hard dry circles. They're as big as dinner plates, but it takes a lot to feed one fire.

Here's the man from the trading post to take our letters. In haste—

Your affectionate sister,

Abigail

June 17. Beside the North Platte River.

Mosquitoes swarmed around Abby's face as she crouched in the sagebrush. Swollen bites already covered every unprotected spot on her body, and now she was completely vulnerable, squatting in the shelter of Emma and Mother's skirts. They stood with their backs to her, while the wide bolts of calico cast circular shadows on the ground. Abby tried to pretend she was in some private, quiet place, but the sound of men shouting close by made her wish she could shrink into a tiny ball and disappear.

Ever since early morning, she had felt a dull, numb

cramping in the pit of her stomach. She was afraid of dysentery and tried to ignore it. But now, as she pulled up her drawers, she saw bloodstains on the faded white cloth. Her mind whirled. That explained the sticky feeling of the last few hours, and her queasiness after the noon break.

"Abigail," Mother called, over her shoulder. "Are you ready?"

"One minute," Abby said, her voice almost a croak. She straightened her petticoat under her dress. Should she tell Mother? She opened her mouth, then changed her mind, running away from the two women as if she'd been stung. Why, *why* did this have to happen now?

"Abigail!" Mother called.

Abby ignored her and ran wildly over the sharp, stubbled ground. She'd been warned about this. Caroline had explained in a hushed, embarrassed voice how women "come around" every month. Mother made veiled comments sometimes when she noticed Abby's dresses were too tight across the bodice. But Abby assumed this would never happen to *her*. Certainly not here, so far from home, in the midst of strangers.

Everyone will know, she thought. Everyone. She slowed to a walk, grateful for the dingy green pattern of her dress. It would hide any stains.

Will stood beside the supply wagon, holding Suzy. "Abby!" he called. "She's ready for you."

Abby climbed into her own wagon as though she were deaf, pulled the cover tight, and pinned it shut. She couldn't face anyone now, especially her brother. In fact, she might not look at any man, ever again.

Her face was on fire. Somewhere, in the deep pocket of her memory, she heard Caroline say, "It's not so bad, once you're used to it. Easier than having a baby."

Abby searched frantically in her trunk for her torn apron and wished she could scream at her sister. Not so bad? *You* never had to wash your rags in a dirty river, with men watching. *You* could talk to Mother easily. I can't.

Abby found the apron, tore the cloth into strips, and stuffed one thick, wadded piece into her drawers, glancing furtively around to be certain she was alone. Then she huddled on the mattress, wondering what to do next.

It's all Pa's fault, she thought wildly. If he hadn't made us follow him, this would have happened at home.

Her heart raced. She heard angry shouts outside and stood up, her head knocking against strings of dried buffalo meat.

"The Lord demands a day of rest!" Uncle Joseph was yelling. "Nothing keeps us from stopping here tomorrow and reading the Scripture."

"Suit yourself."

Abby recognized Mr. Grey's voice and sighed. Would they fight this way until they reached California?

"We need to beat the snow in the mountains," Mr. Grey continued. "Stay and rest with your *womenfolk*," he snarled. "We *men* will move ahead."

Abby was sick of Mr. Grey's rude references to the

Parker women. She pulled on her socks and boots while the argument continued. Captain Foster's low, intense voice cut through the shouting.

"Come, come," he said, clapping his hands. "Parker's right. Our oxen need recruitment. We'll never make it over the mountains at all if we don't rest them. This company camps here tomorrow, and whoever leaves forfeits his share of our provisions."

Just the sound of the men's voices made Abby ashamed of her condition all over again. She longed to find some private place, a spot where she could hide from the burning glances of the miners. She slipped through the cover at the far end of the wagon. Everyone was huddled around her uncle and the captain. She jumped to the ground and stood still for a moment wondering which way to go.

Hundreds of travelers crawled along the trail to the north, looking, she supposed, for a better campsite than this dusty gully. The river lay somewhere beyond; she knew that. Behind her, to the south, a ridge of low bluffs rose from the prairie. She could hide there until dark fell and then come out. Mother would worry, but that couldn't be helped. It wasn't the first time she'd gone off alone.

She walked slowly away from the wagons, careful not to attract attention, and stopped when she heard Mother say in a clear, calm voice, "Wait a moment. If we have a day of rest, I insist we move from this wretched spot. I have no intention of sleeping or eating in filth. We Parkers will fill our water barrels and camp at the foot of the bluffs, where we can observe the Sabbath in peace."

"You're right, ma'am." It sounded like Frank Watson, who liked to stand watch with Will and Matthew. "I'm cook for my mess tonight, and I won't do it here."

"No need to lie in someone else's garbage," added another.

Abby hurried away. If everyone moved to the bluffs, she wanted to get there first. She covered her mouth as she reached the edge of the campground. The stench of rotting food, human waste, and animal dung was pungent. Mother's right, she thought. It *is* filthy.

Abby ran, avoiding hunks of rusted metal and broken dishes. There were signs of people everywhere, and reminders of death: three gravestones tilted behind piles of sod, hastily thrown into mounds.

When she reached the foot of the bluff, she slowed to a walk. She wished she could run away from herself. She hated her long, pointed feet, pinched inside her boots; her tight sleeves, with her wrists jutting out the bottom; the strange new feeling of breasts pressing inside her bodice. Even her head felt different, as though her new shape had crept into her thoughts and left them in disarray.

She scrambled to the top of the bluff, trying to ignore the rags chafing between her legs. When she stood on the flat table, the scene below was so startling she forgot her discomfort. Twin lines of wagons crawled like obedient bugs on both sides of the river. The Platte lay twisted in dark ribbons, weaving a wet pattern through the browns and greens of sagebrush. Her own company was moving, straggling in small groups away from the river.

To the south, the prairie lay empty and untouched. To the west, the river glistened, and when she followed its winding track to the horizon, she saw a dusky line mounded at the sky's rim. Mountains? Abby squinted and held her breath. Maybe it was only a cloudbank— but no, the few clouds today were white and tall; these were hills, the first mountains of the journey.

The prairie was no longer infinite. Abby opened her mouth, swallowed the wind, stretched her arms wide, and began to twirl. She growled, then roared, then whooped. Cries burst from her chest and scraped past her throat as she flung them to the sky. She spun on top of the bluff until the cluttered prairie whirled below her, then sank to the ground and lay spread-eagled, panting. Her insides felt clean, as though emptied of some foul-tasting poison. She lay still, listening to her heart race, smelling the hot, sun-baked grass. She began to hear sounds in layers: the muffled thumps of the wagons, coming toward the bluff, the insistent rumble of the caravan in the distance, and then, suddenly: footsteps.

Her skin prickled, and she jumped up. An Indian woman appeared on the crest of the hill. She was dressed in deerskin decorated with beads. Jet-black braids hung to her waist, and she carried a crude bundle under one arm. She walked straight up to Abby and stood about an arm's length away, staring at her with curious, dancing eyes.

Abby was embarrassed. The woman must have heard her screams; might have seen her whirling around. Abby fingered Pa's knife, lying smooth and secret in her pocket, and glanced furtively behind her. But the young woman seemed to be alone.

Abby cleared her throat. "Hello," she said, forcing a smile.

The woman said nothing, just nodded her head slowly. She reached out and plucked the chain holding Abby's watch. Then she touched the package under her arm. "Swap?" she asked.

Abby clutched the chain and pulled away, shaking her head. "Can you talk to me?" she said.

The woman raised her eyebrows, posing her own silent question. Her dark eyes strayed over Abby's body. Abby felt as if the woman could see through her clothing, but she held her ground and returned the stare.

The woman set her package down, a bundle of rush-like leaves wrapped around a long, dead fish. Its sharp, heady smell assaulted Abby's nose. The woman pointed to the fish and smiled, gesturing for Abby to come closer.

Abby bent to touch the fish, keeping a close watch on the woman from the corner of her eye. The fish was firm, with bright eyes. Abby looked up at the woman. "You caught it?"

The Indian's face was placid, yet curious. She pointed

at the fish, then at Abby's feet. "Swap?"

The woman wanted her boots. Abby's mind raced. Her shoes pinched her; they were broken at the heels. This was her second summer wearing them; they'd been Will's before that. She'd wear through them before she reached California, but she couldn't go barefoot.

What if she refused? The woman looked strong; her movements were graceful but firm. Was it safe to say no?

The woman shifted from one foot to the other, and Abby noticed her moccasins. They covered her ankles and rose to the fringe of her leggings. Intricate beadwork crisscrossed the front, beneath pointed pieces of decoration.

The slippers looked soft and supple, yet sturdy. Abby could imagine kicking Timothy, feeling his skin ripple right through the deerskin. She pulled up her skirt and pointed at her boots, then put a finger on the moccasins. "Swap," she said.

The woman ran her hands over Abby's feet. Abby felt like a horse at auction, but she stood quietly, waiting, trying to hide her longing. The woman's thick braids trailed on the ground. Abby wished she could hold one; feel its weight settle in her hand. Her own hair felt thin and limp at the nape of her neck.

The woman sat down, pulled off her slippers, and held them out to Abby. "Swap," she said.

Abby laughed. What a funny conversation, all based on one word! She unlaced her boots. The woman copied her, like an image in a mirror. They were still a moment, holding their footwear while the wind tugged at Abby's skirts and flicked the fringes on the woman's leggings.

At last, Abby held out her boots. The woman took them and examined the round, reinforced eyelets. She nodded, spoke a few strange, solemn words, then placed the moccasins carefully in Abby's hands. She pointed to the fish, spoke again, and disappeared, carrying the boots under her arm.

Abby let her breath out in a rush. She felt as though she had put herself back together again on the bluff. And somehow, in the remaking, she was different inside. She felt fragile—but strangely calm. Perhaps it's all right to grow up, Abby thought.

She pulled on the moccasins. They were snug and warm. Abby wrapped the fish in its leaves and ran down the bluff to the jumbled confusion of wagons. When she spotted Uncle Joseph, she hurtled toward him, laughing when he crossed his arms over his chest.

"And where have *you* been?" he barked when she came closer. "Should we chain you to the wagon?"

Abby took a deep breath, all the way to the calm place within her stormy heart. "I was busy," she said. "I went hunting. I caught a fish, and some moccasins."

The rest of the family drew close. Uncle Joseph's face reddened, but Abby ignored it. She unwrapped the fish and held it out to him. "Here," she said. "A present, for you." She pulled up her skirts to show off her feet. "Look!"

"Abigail!" Mother hissed. "Drop your skirts. Where did you find those dreadful slippers? And where are your boots?"

"I traded them to an Indian woman. They're *not* dreadful. My boots were too small. They cramped my toes. Anyway," she admitted, "I was afraid to say no. I thought she might hurt me."

"You did the right thing," Uncle Joseph said, and he began to laugh, such an unexpected, harsh sound that Abby jumped.

"Abigail, you never stop surprising me," he said. "I wouldn't be surprised if the Indian woman was afraid of *you*. Look at this, Will," he said, pointing at Abby's feet. "Bear's teeth. Won't she be the envy of every man on the train?"

Abby opened her mouth and closed it. No one said a word. Then Mother laughed. "Why, Abigail. I do believe you've pleased your uncle Joseph!"

A tentative calm expanded inside Abby, growing warm and elastic. She held up the fish and smiled, feeling brave and shy all at once. "Heat some buffalo chips!" she cried. "Supper in an hour!"

June 27. In the Black Hills.

A thick cloud scudded across the moon's face. Abby stood still a moment, waiting for Emma, and watched the bulky shadows of wagons crawl slowly up the trail.

A wolf's howl floated above her, plaintive and high-pitched. The rocks on the south side of the trail kicked the sound back, allowing the wolf to create his own duet.

"Abby?" Emma's voice was anxious.

"Right here."

"I'm afraid. Aren't you?"

Abby waited until her eyes could pick out Emma's blurred form stumbling toward her on the trail. "A little," Abby said. The wolf howled again, closer this time. The dark, mournful notes penetrated Abby's spine and crawled, prickling, up into her skull.

"He won't come after us," Abby said firmly, to convince herself. "But we'd better catch up to the wagons, just the same."

The cloud sailed past the moon; silver shadows glinted on the canvas covers ahead. "We're climbing," Abby said as they hurried over sharp stones. "Can you feel it?"

"Yes," said Emma, her breathing quick and shallow. "It's been hard walking, ever since Fort Laramie. And what dry, desolate country this is at night!"

Abby nodded and pulled her shawl close around her. Neither one of them spoke for a while; traveling in the dark required silence and concentration. Men, oxen, and wagons all moved ahead of them in a subdued rumble. Even Mr. Grey, who was most likely to curse at his animals, had been quiet since nightfall, letting his whip twist and dangle like a snake above the road.

Abby moved as if sleepwalking, placing one soft moc-

casin before the other while the day's events passed before her in a dream. She thought with detached interest
about their barren campground this morning, where
the oxen pawed the hard dirt and balked when the men
hitched them without feed. Abby's stomach growled;
she knew how they felt. She hadn't eaten since noon,
when Matthew came into the campground with a hare.

He'd been gone all morning and had slipped back
silently. They were only aware of him when they heard
his low, tuneless whistle as he cut up the hare, tearing
the skin deftly away from the flesh. He'd been remote,
almost cold, for days. Abby could hardly remember the
way his eyes used to twinkle below his hat brim. Had
she said something wrong?

Since their discovery on Chimney Rock, Abby ex-
pected Matthew to spend time with her, planning
Molly's rescue. But he was more secretive than ever,
disappearing so often that Abby found herself waiting
anxiously for him to come back.

"Abby?" Emma's voice was even more distant. Abby
stood beside a scrubby pine until she heard her aunt's
brisk steps behind her.

"Emma—I'm here."

"Sorry. I'm slower than I'd like."

Abby peered at her aunt. The moon cast flickering
shadows onto her high cheekbones and highlighted the
smooth half-circles of hair around her face.

"Let's walk together," Emma said. "The trail's wider
here."

Abby nodded. The rocks had pulled back from the

rough road, as if to make way for the wagon trains.

"I'm afraid," Emma said with a small laugh. "I know it's silly—but that wolf set me on edge. It's comforting to hear another voice in the dark." She linked arms with Abby and they walked along together, helping each other over the stony spots. After another silence, Emma squeezed her elbow. "You're so quiet," she said. "Thinking about Matthew?"

Abby bit her lip and wished her thoughts didn't show up so clearly on her face.

"Forgive me," Emma said. "I didn't mean to pry. I only wanted to share confidences."

Emma's eyes were dark and appealing in the silver light, but Abby was reluctant to talk. Matthew's secret was tangled up in her thoughts like stockings lost in the bedclothes. It would be so easy to give everything away. At the same time, she was tired of protecting Matthew. He wouldn't even speak to her lately, while Emma waited patiently to be her friend. Maybe she could share something, yet still keep her promise.

"You're not prying," Abby said at last.

Emma's peal of laughter filled the shadows and warmed the night air. "Yes, I am! I'm as curious about Matthew as anyone. But I wouldn't dream of breaking your confidence with him."

Abby stared at her aunt. How much did she know?

Emma laughed softly. "Just answer yes or no. Does Matthew have a secret? Some special reason for coming with us?"

Abby smiled. She could answer that. "Yes."

"And you know why?"

"Yes."

"But you've promised not to tell."

"That's right."

They both laughed and hurried along the trail. Abby's feet almost skipped in her moccasins. What a relief to share things—even partway.

"I've been wondering why you wouldn't talk to me," Emma said softly. "I thought I might be too proper for you."

"Oh, no!" Abby cried. "It wasn't that at all. I was afraid I'd give something away. I'm not very good at keeping secrets," she explained. "Besides, I thought *you* didn't want to talk to *me*—because I was wild and unladylike."

Emma's musical laugh echoed off the rocks. "Believe it or not, I envy you. I know how to ride, but I don't think your uncle would allow it, not in my condition. Sometimes I hate these skirts, and my big belly, and my hands just so in my mitts, and my bonnet ever so carefully placed on my head." Emma's tone was prissy. She swept her sunbonnet up onto her coiled hair and settled it there, blinking primly beneath the brim.

"Emma!" Abby cried. "Don't you want to be a lady?"

"Part of me does," Emma admitted. "But sometimes, when you go riding off on Timothy, I wish I could go too."

"We'll do it, then," Abby promised. "Someday. When Chester's free and Uncle Joseph is *very* busy."

Emma laughed. The moon disappeared again, and

they stumbled on up the trail.

"I'm glad you and Matthew have an understanding," Emma said suddenly. "It's nice to have sweethearts on the journey."

"What do you mean?" Abby couldn't control the trembling in her voice. "There's nothing between Matthew and me."

"Abby!" Emma laughed. "It's written all over your faces."

"That's not fair," Abby cried. "He won't even *talk* to me. When I say something, he pretends I'm not there." Abby was close to tears. Was this what friendship with Emma would mean—a gentle prying until her insides were scooped out?

"Dear Abigail," Emma said. "Don't be upset. It's all right if you care for him."

"I *don't*." Abby twisted away from Emma's hand.

"Abby, don't go away. We're just jealous, that's all, your mother and I."

Abby whirled on Emma. "Jealous? Of what?"

"Did you ever see your uncle look at me that way? As if he'd like to scoop me up on his horse and throw me over his saddle? It's like the song about the fair lady who gives up her house and home 'to go with the gypsy Davey.'" Emma began to hum the tune, and then she laughed. "I wish your uncle would do that to me. But he'd have a time hoisting me up there, the way my belly is now."

Abby was shocked. Her aunt's eyes danced and shone, reflecting the moonlight.

"You see, I'm not as proper as you think," Emma said. "Now, come on. Don't be mad. We'll catch up to the train and chat. And I promise, no more questions about Matthew. It's your turn—ask me something, anything you like."

Abby slowly calmed down. She remembered her loneliness, a few weeks ago, when she'd discovered the changes in her body and tried to run away. Maybe she could talk to Emma about these things, the way she did with Caroline.

"All right," Abby said boldly. "Tell me about your wedding night. Were you afraid?"

"Of course," Emma said. "I was terrified." She laughed. "My mother warned me not to sleep in my husband's arms. She said it was bad luck." Emma lowered her voice. "I broke all the rules that night," she admitted. "And the next night, too. Joseph's different, underneath his gruff talk." She looked at Abby apologetically, as if her loyalties were torn. Then she gave her belly a gentle pat. "I guess that's why I'm in the soup now."

Abby was delighted. Caroline had never talked to her that way. Would Emma tell her everything she longed to know about men and women? She wanted to ask more, but she heard the men ahead shouting, "Halt! Halt!"

"Wait," Emma said as Abby started forward. "Promise you'll talk to me again."

"Of course," Abby said. "And I'm sorry I was cross,"

she whispered. "You were right—I *do* like him a little."
She squeezed Emma's hand. "Let's go," she said.
"Maybe Uncle Joseph is waiting to carry you away."

They giggled and hurried toward the wagons, where
they found Timothy standing by the trail, his reins dangling on the ground. "Mother?" Abby called. The
canvas flapped; no one answered. Everyone was gathered around an abandoned wagon that sat beside the
trail. Men shifted silently as a bulky form appeared
from the black interior and filled the circular opening. A
woman's round face caught the moonlight.

"Visitors! Why, how nice!" There was a sudden, jostling movement as Mother untangled herself from the
crowd and peered at the stranger.

"Praise the Lord!" the woman cried. "Another
woman." She said the word with reverence and clasped
her hands together. In spite of her size, she climbed
nimbly from the wagon box to the ground and stretched
out her round arms. "I'm Sarah Walker," she said,
grasping Mother's hands.

"Mary Parker," Mother said. "Pleased to meet you."

The two women gazed fondly at each other like long-
lost friends. Honestly, Abby thought. You'd think they
were in a parlor, instead of on a rocky trail in the middle of nowhere.

"Are you all alone?" Mother asked.

"My husband, James, is with me," Sarah Walker explained. "He's been ill. Our company waited a few days.
When he didn't get better, they left us to fend for our-

selves. I refused to make him travel—I knew it would be the end of him. So I doctored him. I'm sure he can travel tomorrow."

How can she be so cheerful? Abby wondered. Abandoned by her friends, left to die in this dry spot, without water or feed. What kind of people would do that?

"Cowards," Mary Parker said, as if Abby had spoken out loud. "No decent man would do such a thing. Well, don't you worry, Mrs. Walker. You can join us. I'm sure our captain will agree."

"Not so fast!" Mr. Grey shouted as Captain Foster stepped forward. "What's wrong with the husband? Maybe it's cholera. They might have had good reason to leave them behind."

"None of that," Mrs. Walker said firmly. "There's been no cholera since Fort Laramie. He's got a bad case of the camp sickness, and it's weakened him." She smiled at Mr. Grey. "I dare say you might have run into it yourself."

"That's true," said the captain, touching his hat. "It strikes everyone, sometime. Ma'am, we'd be pleased to take you along."

"Thank you for your kindness," Sarah Walker said.

In the silence that followed, hoofbeats rang on the stones. A few men raised their guns as a tall figure on a bony mule slid like a snake from behind the boulders.

"Halt!" Uncle Joseph cried. "Who goes?"

"Don't trouble, now," a rough voice replied. "This one's friendly, he is, just hauling peltries to Fort Laramie."

Abby couldn't tell if this second stranger was part Indian; a Spaniard or American. He was dressed in torn, faded deerskin; his hair hung loose on his shoulders, and an old hat shielded his eyes. A stout pony stood beside the mule, shifting uneasily beneath a sloping pile of furs that glistened in the moonlight.

"Leave off the guns," the man said, rubbing his sharp nose with the back of his hand. "This old bird's too tough for your dinner."

Captain Foster lowered his rifle and motioned to the others to do the same. "I'm the captain of this company. Foster's the name." When the man said nothing, he asked, "You come from the west?"

"Bear River. Trapped there all winter. Beaver's going, with all you corncrackers about." He ignored the soft muttering from the crowd, continuing to insult them in a matter-of-fact way. "You're taking it all. Buffalo, antelope, beaver. Soon be nothing left for mountain men like me, or the Indians that own this land. Greed, that's what it is." He spat loudly, then added, "Well, this one's off to Laramie. Sell my furs. Then hire with more of you greenhorns, back to the mountains."

His speech was as gnarled as his hands, which lay still and relaxed on the mule's withers. Abby drew closer and studied his moccasins. They matched her own.

"Women!" the trapper exclaimed, catching sight of her. "There's more ahead, too. How'll you get *them* over the mountains?"

Just as Abby felt a retort swelling inside, Uncle Joseph stepped forward. "These women are doing fine," he said. "Better than some men I could mention." He glanced toward Herbert Grey.

Emma was right, Abby thought. There *is* another side to Uncle Joseph.

"They'll make it," her uncle was saying. He put out his hand and shook the trapper's twisted fingers. "Joseph Parker. What's ahead?"

"There's feed around the bend, where the trail widens. You'd best stop there. Pulled over myself, but then I got curious. Heard your voices. Wagons backed up all the way to the crossing, and no grass beyond."

"We're near the ferry?" the captain asked.

"You are. But there's a wait to go over. Mormons take in money all day long, ferrying. Some folks swim—and drown. How many are you?"

"A dozen wagons. Thirteen, with Mrs. Walker," Uncle Joseph said.

"Hold on," Herbert Grey growled, pushing to the front of the crowd. "I say thirteen wagons are bad luck."

"Then perhaps you'd rather go on alone and leave us with an even dozen again," Captain Foster said dryly.

The men laughed, and Mr. Grey slipped away into the shadows, muttering angrily.

"We'll pull up ahead," the captain said, waving to the crowd. "Take your animals to feed. Frank Watson—you here?"

"Yes, sir." Frank stepped toward them, and tipped his hat.

"Help Mrs. Walker. Hitch up her mules, drive them if she wants." He turned to the trapper. "We thank you for your advice. Good luck to you."

The crowd broke up as men returned to their wagons and whipped up their oxen. The Parker family hesitated near the bony mule, and Uncle Joseph said, "If you'd like to rest with us tonight and share our fire, we'd be pleased to feed you in the morning—wouldn't we, Mary?"

Mother nodded. "You're welcome to join us," she said. "You too, Mrs. Walker."

The trapper hesitated and removed his hat. "Forgive my rudeness, ma'am," he said. "This one calls it a treat to enjoy real cooking." His eyes fell on Abby, and he blinked twice. "Any girl found herself a pair of parfleche moccasins got to be a bit unusual. You steal those?" he asked.

Abby drew closer. His deeply creased face shone in the moonlight; she realized he meant to be friendly. She smiled. "I traded my boots for these moccasins, and a fish."

The trapper laughed. "Take you with me, I would," he said. "You interested? Always need someone to make friends with the Indians."

"She's not going anywhere." Matthew appeared from the shadows and stood below the trapper, both hands on his hips.

Abby glared at him. Since when do you decide what I can do? she wanted to ask, but she said nothing.

The trapper grinned. "Beg pardon. You her young man?"

Abby wished the hills would cave in around her, but

Matthew just shrugged. He seemed eager to question the trapper. "Did you say there were other women ahead?" he asked.

"There are. Can't say I got a close look. This one keeps his distance."

"Pardon me." Sarah Walker pushed toward them. "There was a young woman in my train."

Matthew wheeled on her and grasped her by the wrists, staring hungrily into her eyes. "Tell me about her," he demanded.

"Reed!" Uncle Joseph barked, but Emma tugged his sleeve and put a finger to her lips.

"A sweet young girl," Mrs. Walker said. "She begged the men to wait for me. I think she'd have stayed herself, if her companion hadn't pulled her away. She called them cowards, murderers—but it didn't do any good."

Matthew released Sarah Walker's wrists and let his arms dangle by his sides. "What was her name?" he whispered.

"Molly. Molly Reed. A pretty girl, full of spunk, but too young to be on her own. You know her?"

No one spoke. Abby heard wagons start up, and the crack of a whip, but it seemed distant, like sounds drifting over still water.

"Yes," Matthew whispered at last. "I do. She's my sister."

June 29. Lower Ferry, North Platte River.

"Abigail! Where are you?"

"Over here!" Abby followed the sound of her mother's voice until she reached the outskirts of the crowd. Mother stood beside Sarah Walker, her face gaunt with worry.

"Where's Matthew?" Mother called.

"I don't know. Why, what's wrong?" Abby cried.

"I'm afraid I've done something foolish." Sarah Walker had to raise her soft voice to be heard above the tumult. "I told Matthew his sister must be just ahead. He borrowed our horse to go look for her. Now I've learned Molly's party went on to the second ferry a few days ago. They'll be miles beyond us." Mrs. Walker's cheeks grew flushed as her words tumbled out. "I'm afraid he's just foolish enough to try and swim the horse over. The gelding's strong, but this current is fierce."

Abby searched the crowd frantically. A seething mass of men, oxen, mules, and wagons surged along the banks of the North Platte, and the crush of wagons arriving from behind seemed as if it might push everyone headlong into the river. "I'll find him!" she shouted.

"Wait!" Mother cried, but Abby darted away, bumping into arms, shoulders, and hands as she searched the crowd for Matthew. She clutched her elbows to her side, trying to make herself invisible. Closer to the bank, where the Mormon ferries were competing with homemade rafts, the crush was nearly impenetrable.

"Excuse me," Abby begged, looking for wedges of light between leather coats and buckskin jackets. As she bumped and jostled her way through, men whistled, laughed, and used words that made her skin crawl. The crowd seemed to close in on her as she edged closer to the river.

Suddenly, she was out in the open, gulping for air as if she'd been under water too long. She stood still a moment, wavering, her eyes scanning the bank. It would be easy to lose everyone here, to miss one's turn on the ferry and wander forever among a thousand strangers. Abby was tempted to retreat to the Parker wagons when she recognized her brother's voice shouting hoarsely: "Matthew. Wait!"

Abby ran upstream, her feet slipping in the mud. She couldn't see Will in the confusion on the shore, but she caught sight of Matthew's familiar gray hat bobbing a few inches above the crowd. Abby slid to the edge of the coffee-colored water.

"Matthew!" she screamed. He was climbing onto the Walker's black gelding, urging it forward before he was even settled in the saddle. He flailed his heels against the animal's sides. The horse tossed his wide head, fighting the bit.

"Matthew!" Abby called again, above the roar on the bank. "Molly's not here. She's at the other ferry!" But a second commotion drowned her words. A homemade raft, made of four dugout canoes lashed together, had pushed away from the shore with a wagon on board. Two men were fighting, balanced precariously on the gunwales of the outside canoe. One was Mr. Jones from their caravan.

"Trying to steal across?" his opponent shouted. "I'll show you what we do with stowaways." And before Abby could cry out, Mr. Jones was thrown overboard.

"I can't swim!" he cried desperately, his arms thrashing the water. The river sucked him away as five or six men plunged after him. They struggled against the current, pulled downstream toward the gelding's churning legs.

"Get that horse out of here," one of the men snarled at Matthew. "Can't you see there's a man under water?"

Matthew's face was white with fear. He drew back on the gelding. The black horse, his shoulders foaming with sweat, reared up. Abby watched in horror as Matthew fell in a backward arc over the horse's withers and into the current.

Abby was in the water before she knew what she was doing. Her skirt tangled around her ankles as she stumbled toward Matthew, who floundered just beyond her, trying to regain his balance.

"Abby, watch it!" Will, appearing out of nowhere, grabbed her arm as the gelding's rear hoof caught Matthew full in the chest with a hollow thud.

The river bottom shifted beneath Abby like something alive, sucking her feet out from under her. For a few seconds, the wet, roiling dark closed over her. Then she came up sputtering and choking, with Will's arm clutching her waist. "Steady," he said, tugging her back. "It's like quicksand here." They struggled out of the current toward the bank. Beside them, two strangers were dragging Matthew onto the muddy shore, where they laid him, white and senseless, on some wide planks before rushing back to the river.

Abby and Will stumbled up the bank and stood looking down on Matthew. Water poured from their clothes; they were both shaking with cold.

Matthew opened his eyes. Their gray irises matched the pallor of his face. He coughed and spat up blood. "Can you prop me up a bit?" he whispered.

Will stood transfixed, his eyes sharp with anger. When he made no move to help, Abby dragged a nearby sack of cornmeal to Matthew's head, gently lifted his shoulders, and slid the bag beneath him.

Matthew groaned, pointed to his chest, and began to cough again. Abby looked up at Will, pleading silently for help. But he turned away in disgust.

"I'd better have a look," Abby said softly. She unbuttoned Matthew's shirt, her fingers trembling when they met his cold skin. She gasped. Across his lower ribs, the horse had left a raw, perfect imprint of his hoof.

Will sucked in his breath but kept his arms locked tight across his chest, spinning to stare at Abby in disbelief as she slowly peeled Matthew's shirt open to reveal the whole wound.

"I don't dare touch it," she whispered. "It's a big welt. I think we'd better find Mother and Mrs. Walker. They'll know what to do." She pulled the fabric gently back together, letting her wet hair fall across her face to hide her embarrassment.

When Matthew tried to sit up, lines of pain whipped across his face like lashes from a whip. "Feels like a broken rib," he coughed.

"That's the least of our problems," Will said, pacing angrily in front of them. "At least you're alive. If you hadn't been such a fool, we might have saved Mr. Jones." He pointed toward the river, where a line of men moved against the current, their arms linked, their eyes fixed on the murky water. "And who knows how we'll ever catch the Walkers' horse." Will gestured upstream. The black gelding stood snorting and stamping his forelegs, while a small crowd of men circled warily around him.

Abby had forgotten about Mr. Jones. "You think he drowned?" she whispered. "But that wasn't Matthew's fault. Mr. Jones was a stowaway on that raft. Someone pushed him in. He couldn't swim."

"You'll say anything to defend Matthew, won't you?" Will hissed. He turned on his heel.

"Wait!" Matthew cried. "Will, I'm sorry. I thought this was my last chance—" Another spasm of coughing shook him.

Will slammed his fist into an open palm. "If you had listened to me," he said slowly, his face red with anger, "you'd have known it was pointless. Molly's not even at this crossing. Her party went on to the next ferry days ago. You might as well give up."

Matthew's eyes widened with shock. He looked

pleadingly at Abby. She nodded. "Mrs. Walker told me the same thing," she said. "That's why I tried to stop you."

Matthew groaned. He shuddered and closed his eyes.

"Matthew?" Abby listened to his breathing. It was rough and uneven. She hesitated, then slipped one hand under his matted hair, pushed the sack of grain away, and lowered his head gently to the rough planks.

"You do that so well," Will said bitterly. "Any excuse to touch him."

"Will," Abby warned. She looked quickly at Matthew, to see if he had heard, but his face was still. "We've got to get help," she said.

Will pulled her aside roughly, keeping his eyes on Matthew's motionless form. Abby jerked her hand away. "Will, what's wrong?"

"How do you think I feel?" Will said. "You knew about his sister all along. I thought we were in this to-gether. Well, this time, *I've* got the secret." His face grew dark.

"What?" Abby asked quickly. Her hands were sweaty, in spite of the chills rippling up and down her back.

"I don't see why I should tell you," Will said at last. "And I know how you feel about Matthew," he added in a tight, choked voice. "I watched you unbuttoning his shirt. You loved every minute of it. But you'd better watch yourself."

"Will!" Molly protested. "He's hurt. I just wanted to see what was wrong."

"Oh, come on," Will said in disbelief. He turned to the river. The line of men had given up; they dropped hands and staggered out of the current with their heads bent, as if ashamed of their failure.

"That's it for Mr. Jones," Will said grimly. He pulled himself up tall and stared at Abby, as if seeing her for the first time. "Go change your clothes," he ordered. "And find Mother. I'll wait here with Matthew." When Abby hesitated, he cried hoarsely, "Go on. You think I'll hurt him? Get something decent on!"

Abby glanced down, suddenly aware of the revealing way her dress clung to her bodice and waist. She blushed deeply and ran, dodging men and animals again, searching desperately for their own wagons. When she finally found her mother, she blurted out her news, pointed to the area where Matthew lay, and scrambled into their wagon before Mother could speak to her, quickly closing the canvas to blot out the world. She peeled her wet clothes from her shivering body, then pulled on her only other dress, a faded green calico.

Tears fell unchecked as she fumbled with her buttons. When she was dressed, she jumped down and slipped behind their wagons. If she made a wide circle around the ferry crowd, perhaps she could find her way back to Matthew without jostling through the thousands of jeering eyes that seemed to follow her everywhere.

Just beyond the Parker wagons she heard hoofbeats behind her, but she ignored them. She didn't want to see anyone just now.

"Morning, Indian Trader."

Abby whirled around and nearly bumped into the trapper's mule. The wiry man sat easily on his mount, one leg gripping the rope of his pack pony.

"Greetings," he said.

Abby managed a smile. The twang in his voice fascinated her; so did the life he had described: hunting and trapping alone in the mountains, all winter long. "Hello," she said. "You surprised me."

He tapped his chest. "This one bring those tears?"

Abby shook her head and brushed the back of her hand across her face. "No, not you. We've had some trouble. One man drowned, and our friend—Matthew Reed—was hurt trying to get across the river. He's trying to find his sister—" Abby gulped and was quiet. Why should this stranger be interested in any of this? But he nodded his head slowly and sympathetically.

"River's got a bottom that moves," he said. "Pulls you down."

Abby smiled weakly. "I know. I got wet myself."

They studied each other for a minute, and Abby noticed that his furs were gone. In their place were bulging saddlebags and tools. "You've been to the fort and back already?" she asked.

He grinned, showing gaps in his teeth. "Nope. Found someone going home. Said he'd 'seen the elephant.' Traded me all his tools and supplies for my furs. I'll go twenty miles for every one you greenhorns take. This one'll find his own private spot to cross the Platte, be in

Bear River Valley weeks before you. Find some quiet again."

Abby had a sudden inspiration. "Do we all follow the same route from here?"

"Don't know," he said. "Some take Sublette's Cut-off. Some go to Salt Lake, needing provisions. Which way you going?"

"Sublette's, I think," Abby said. The name was familiar; Captain Foster had discussed it with her uncle. "If you go that way"—Abby hesitated, then blurted—"could you look for someone?"

"Maybe. Don't like to mix too closely with all you people. Too much crowding."

"Then why are you here?" Abby teased, hoping she didn't sound rude.

"Couldn't help it." A tiny smile caught one side of the trapper's mouth and pulled it up. "Got curious about my Indian Trader and her family." His piercing gaze, which should have frightened her, was oddly reassuring.

"Do you think you could get curious about someone else?" Abby asked carefully.

The trader shrugged. "Could be. Depends who it is."

"Matthew's sister. She's the reason for all the trouble this morning," Abby started to explain. "Please, wait right here. I want to show you something. Don't go away."

She ran to their supply wagon, hoisted herself over the wheel, and searched among the bags and barrels until she found Matthew's pack. She jumped down, holding it up high, and hurried back to the trader. "I know it's here," she said, rummaging boldly through Matthew's things until her fingers closed around a hard, square packet.

"Look." She pulled out the daguerreotype, unhooked the tiny latch, and set it on the trapper's knee. "Remember, when you first met us—Mrs. Walker told Matthew Reed that she knew his sister?"

"Sure. Upset him some, didn't it?"

Abby nodded. "This is Molly Reed. Will you look for her?"

The trapper tipped the frame to find the picture. "Pretty thing," he said. "The way her brother's behaving, seems she must have man trouble."

Abby nodded. "I'm afraid so."

The trapper pulled off his hat. His hair fell in limp strands onto his collar as he scratched his scalp. "Say I find her. Then what? Can't steal her myself. It's no place for a woman, where this one's going."

If any other man had talked to her this way, Abby would have been embarrassed. But the trapper's manner was so straightforward, it didn't bother her. "Tell her..." She hesitated, remembering the worry in Mrs. Walker's voice. Molly was in trouble, but Matthew was in no shape to chase after her now. "Tell her friends will come for her. As soon as they can," Abby said at last. It sounded lame, but she didn't know what else to say.

"You helping your young man start a search party?" the trapper asked, smiling.

"He's not my young man!" Abby protested, but she found herself grinning back at him. What a strange friend I've made, she thought.

"Beg pardon. Well, see what I can do for you. Don't find too many ladies on this route. Most are afraid to leave home."

"I'm not," Abby said, tossing her head.

"Nope." The trapper glanced at the daguerreotype once more, then tapped his head. "She's in here, now."

Abby returned the case to Matthew's pack. "Thank you," she said, suddenly feeling shy.

"Pleased to help. Don't like to see ladies in trouble." He frowned, as if remembering something, then shook his finger at her. "Watch the lakes of saleratus, up ahead," he warned.

"Saleratus? Where?"

"In the water. In the ground. Mules know to avoid it. But oxen, now, or cows—they've no sense. When they bleed from the nose, shoot them. It's a kindness." He winked. "Don't you go swimming in that water either."

"Don't worry. After this morning, I don't know if I'll ever swim again."

"You will. Wait until Bear River. Stay out of trouble, now." He clucked to his mule and waved his hand.

"Stop!" Abby cried, running alongside. "I don't even know your name!"

"This one likes it that way," the trapper said. He settled into the saddle, twisting his spine until he seemed fused to the mule. Abby watched their swaying, lop-sided passage around the wagon train. The trapper skirted broken barrels and a dead ox, passed through a cleft in the rocks, and disappeared. Abby heard a whistle; the trapper's head poked up above the jumbled heaps of boulders. With one last, casual wave, he disappeared.

"Abigail Parker!" Mother's sharp voice came from behind her. "Are you waving at a man?"

Abby whirled around. "Maybe," she said vaguely, looking past her mother. Uncle Joseph and Will were moving slowly through the crowd, supporting Matthew between them. He took short, careful steps, each one sending a little jolt of pain across his white face. His shirt was still open, revealing a wide bandage wrapped around his chest. When Abby started toward him, Mother laid a hand on her arm. "Leave him be," she said. "He's got a lot of explaining to do."

"But is he all right?" Abby asked.

Sarah Walker bustled up beside them, her round face glistening. "He's just fine," she said. "A broken rib. It hurts, but it will mend."

Relief warmed Abby like the sun making the shadows dance on the hills. She glanced up at the ridge above her, wondering if the trapper watched them, but nothing moved.

"Who was that strange man?" Mother demanded. "He looked like that trapper we met."

"Don't worry, Mother," Abby said. "He's a friend."

Mother's mouth made a straight, firm line across her face, and her eyes narrowed to a cold blue. "If you want to stay friends with *me*, young lady, you'll remember

what I told you about the men on this trip. I won't have
you flirting with strangers. Seems to me we've had
enough trouble this morning, without you making
more."

Abby bit her lip, but Sarah Walker laughed unexpec-
tedly, her face beaming like a sunflower. "I always did
like a girl with spunk," she said. "Looks like you've got
one on your hands, Mary."

Abby wanted to throw her arms around Mrs. Walker,
to be enveloped in her deep, full chest, but she didn't
dare.

Suddenly, Mother laughed, a soft chuckle. "It's a
blessing you joined us, Sarah," she said. "You remind us
of the sunshine, beyond the gloominess. I should notice
Abigail's light side more often." Mother smiled and
kissed Abby so quickly it was like the soft flicker of a
moth against her cheek. Then her face settled back into
its familiar sternness. "Now come along," she said.
"We're next in line for the ferries."

Abby followed the two women to the wagons. In spite
of everything that had happened, she felt light on her
feet. She slipped her hands into her pockets, as if the
new friends she had made were nestled there, warm
and secret within the curve of her fingers.

July 2, 1850.

Dearest Caroline,

Suzy is dead. She drank poisoned water from the lakes of saleratus. Uncle Joseph rammed salt pork down her throat with his whipstock, as if he were cleaning a gun barrel, but it was too late. She started to bleed from the nose, and he had to shoot her. It was a kindness. We rolled rocks over her body so she wouldn't explode in the sun. I hope there's green grass and trees where she's gone.

Every place I turn here, I find the bloated carcass of a dead animal. The blowing dust always smells of death. No wonder they call the nearest stream "Poison Spider Creek."

The ferry crossing was dreadful. First Mr. Jones drowned, then Matthew broke a rib. We almost lost our wagons because Uncle Joseph didn't want to pay the Mormons $1.50 to ride their ferries. Instead, he borrowed a "boat" made of eight canoes lashed together. The wagons rode on top, and we tied the animals to the side. Some of the oxen swam across, but when they were halfway over, they tried to turn around. The raft started to rock, and I thought we might end up in the water, but we managed to reach the other side.

Matthew still moves very slowly. No one even notices when I drive the oxen or ride Timothy—it takes everyone who can walk to move our cattle up the rocky trail. My moccasins will fall apart before this trip is over.

We are climbing slowly towards South Pass. I will give this letter to a Mormon who is returning to Fort Laramie. It comes with love from

> *your affectionate sister,*
> *Abigail*

July 9. Ice Slough, near the Sweetwater River.

Abby knelt in the long swamp grass, combing the sharp blades with her fingers. Clouds of sand and dust rose with the wind; she licked her cracked lips and rubbed grit from her eyes.

All over the strange bog—a mile of shaggy carpet laid out on a desert landscape—the ground resounded with the sharp thwack of shovels hitting sod. Abby opened her knife and ripped out hunks of grass with her fingers. She stabbed the ground with the knife's blade, but it jarred in her hands; the matted sod was impenetrable. She would have to wait until someone dug down to water. Abby wiped the knife on her skirt and put it away as a shadow fell across her knees.

"Thirsty?" Will stood in front of her, brandishing a shovel. "Let's try this."

Abby scrambled to her feet. "Want me to dig?" She swallowed. The words caught and scraped against her thick tongue. She longed for a drink of water.

"I'll do it," said Will. "I'm waiting on Matthew. Of course, he's much too *weak* to work. Or so he says. He'd be better off looking for his sister. Not that she's worth finding."

"What do you mean by that?" Abby asked sharply.

Will scowled and shook his head, nodding in the direction of the wagons. Abby looked behind her. Matthew was walking toward them with slow, careful steps as though the empty buckets he carried were full to the brim. His body was slightly stooped and concave, his face a pale, washed gray. He set the buckets down beside them. "If you dig deep, you might find something here you don't expect," he said.

"Gold?" Abby asked.

Matthew laughed. "Not exactly. But something valuable."

"Like what?" Will's voice was cold and accusing.

"Dig down," Matthew said. "You'll see."

"I guess you like to see me work," Will said. He stomped on the shovel with one worn boot. The ground beneath sucked at the blade and gave way. "Something's wet down there," he said.

Abby watched her brother dig. Will puzzled her. He knew Matthew's rib still pained him, but he continued to complain about how little he was able to work. All week long, following the Sweetwater River to its source, Will grew more and more sullen. Abby guessed it was more than the tiresome dust or their slow progress through the mountains that annoyed him. He rarely spoke to Matthew, and he refused to tell Abby the secret he claimed to be hiding.

Will removed a circle of sod and began to heave wet soil out of the shallow pit. When he'd dug down about a foot, the shovel rang out against something hard. "Rock!" he grunted.

"Keep digging," Matthew said.

Will looked up. Sweat streaked his wide face. "Whatever you say." He slammed the shovel into the hole. The handle vibrated with the impact. "Here!" He tossed the shovel at Matthew. "Let's see you dig through solid rock."

Matthew took the shovel and turned to Abby. "Stick your hand in there, and tell me what you find."

Abby hesitated and looked at her brother. Will's eyes were a sharp, cold blue. She couldn't read them. She shrugged and slipped her arm into the hole. Her fingers grazed something cold and wet. "What is it?"

Matthew laughed. "Can't you tell?"

Abby explored the pit with her fingers. "It feels like ice!"

"It is."

"But how—" Abby sat back on her heels. "We're in the desert. How can there be ice here? It's so hot!"

"Think how high we are." Matthew's arm swept toward the horizon, where the Wind River Mountains piled range upon snowy range above the barren valley. "We're climbing all the time, even though we can't feel it. The sod keeps the water frozen, like sawdust in an icehouse."

"Let me see." Will grabbed the shovel and plunged

the blade back into the hole. Something cracked, then water spurted from the ground. Will bent over and brought up a sharp slab of ice, covered with mud. Abby snatched it away, rubbed it clean on her skirt, and opened her knife. She chipped off small pieces of ice and passed them out, then sucked eagerly on the dirty chunk in her hand while Will slowly filled the buckets.

"This is something for my scrapbook!" Abby exclaimed. "Ice under the ground, in the middle of summer."

"Scrapbook?" Will tossed another hunk of ice into the pail and stared at her.

"Abby keeps track of all the rivers and streams we pass," Matthew said.

Will pounded the hole with his shovel again. "Excuse me. I forgot you two know everything about each other."

"What do you mean?" Matthew's eyes were pale.

"I mean, I've been watching you. I see how you feel about my sister. But if you want to know, I'll be glad when your blasted rib is healed and you can start running after Molly again. This time, I wouldn't dream of stopping you."

"Will!" Abby gasped.

Her brother's eyes narrowed to slits when he turned on her, gripping the handle of the shovel until his knuckles gleamed. "Not that I understand what you're doing. After all, Molly's lost, whether you find her or not. Once a girl's lived that way—"

Matthew spun Will around by the shoulders and

shook him. "You'd better say what you mean," he
hissed. "If Molly's in some sort of trouble I don't know
about, and you've hidden it from me..." Matthew took
a deep breath and let go of Will's shirt, waiting.

"All right, I'll tell you." Will's voice was tight, the
anger barely controlled. "Your precious sister's not married. Judson Hall has other plans. He'll use her in California, where women are scarce. Such a pretty girl,
she's turned out to be his own personal gold mine." Will
turned and looked Matthew in the face. "Can you understand that? Or shall I embarrass my sister and spell
it out more clearly?"

"You've said enough." Matthew's voice was tense.
"How do you know all this?"

"Mrs. Walker. She thought we'd better keep it quiet,
until you were better." He looked at Abby; her face as
hot as the wind humming through the dry grass. She
took a step backward, but Will followed her, almost
spitting in her face. "Before you get so cozy with
Matthew, you'd better do some thinking," Will hissed.
"How can you love a man who's sister is a *whore?*" The
insult burst hoarsely from some place deep inside him.

A strange, wild light glowed in Matthew's eyes. Abby
screamed as Matthew sprang forward, fists flying. Will
staggered, dropped to one knee, then caught himself.
He ducked his head. When Matthew came at him
again, swinging his arms awkwardly, Will plowed into
Matthew's stomach. They fell with a heavy thud onto
the ground, rolling about in the grass with boots and
fists flailing. Will cursed and grunted, his face a dark

purple, and clutched Matthew around the neck.

Matthew weakened almost immediately, and Abby imagined his ribs broken beyond healing this time. She caught sight of the water bucket. Without hesitating, she grabbed the pail of melting ice, hoisted it to her waist, and sloshed the icy water onto her brother's neck. He yelled hoarsely and rolled to the side. Matthew vomited a thin stream of liquid into the dirt and lay still.

Abby stood between the two of them, not knowing what to do. Will pulled himself to his knees. His blue eyes were sharp with surprise, his thin hair plastered to his forehead. He pulled his hand away from his bleeding mouth and looked down, stunned, at the raw tooth lying in his palm. "My God," he muttered, his words slurring.

Abby gasped. "Oh, Will—"

Matthew lurched to his feet and stared at Will's hand in disbelief. "How could I have done that?" he said brokenly. "I'm as bad as my father."

"Huh?" Will stared at Matthew.

Matthew rubbed his hands over his face as though washing it, then bent to pick up his hat, punching the crown into shape before he spoke.

"When Dad and I were on the riverboat, the same thing happened to him." Matthew's voice was distant, as though coming to them all the way from the Missouri River months ago. "A man insulted my sister; called her . . . that name." He glanced at Abby apologetically, then continued, "Dad went into a rage. He was crazy.

I'd never seen him like that. Someone knocked him across the boat. He smashed into an iron post on the deck and died the next day."

Matthew swayed as though he might faint, and Abby caught his elbow, releasing him when he steadied. "When you started talking about Molly, something snapped inside." Matthew's eyes closed, as if the memory pained him. "I saw everything: Dad lying on the deck of the ship, bleeding, and no one helping him. I remembered the way he looked at me, making me promise that I'd bring Molly home, so Ma wouldn't die of grief. No one would help me dig his grave." He swallowed hard and looked up at Will. "God, Will, I'm sorry. I never meant to hurt you. I forgot who you were; who I was, even."

Abby glanced at her brother to see if he would show any sympathy, but he just shook his head. "You're crazy," Will slurred, spitting into the grass.

"I know I've been nothing but trouble to your family," Matthew continued. "If you'd like, I can be on my way tomorrow."

"Suit yourself," Will said.

The hot wind whistled in the grass, but Abby felt as cold as the ice beneath the sod. "You can't turn him out," she said fiercely. "He was getting better, but look at him now. Can't you see he can hardly walk?"

Matthew held out his hands to both of them. "Please," he whispered. "Forgive me. And don't be enemies. We have no one but each other out here." When Will and Abby kept their arms pinned to their sides, he sighed. "Don't fight with your brother, Abby. He's only trying to take care of you. The way I should have done with my own sister. Kiss and make up." He touched Will's shoulder.

"Kiss her yourself." Will jumped away as if stung. "That's what you want, isn't it?"

He wheeled away from them, picked up the empty pail and shovel, and limped off through the sagebrush.

"Will!" Abby cried. Tears streamed down her face as she stumbled after him. Matthew caught her by the arm; she staggered and lost her balance. "Let me go!" she shrieked.

Matthew's fingers dug into her skin. "I won't let this ruin everything," he said. Abby twisted and squirmed, but he held firm, although his hands were shaking. "Abby, look at me." He turned her toward him. Abby couldn't look into his eyes. She stared at a wooden button, hanging by one thread from his faded shirt.

"Molly's not the kind of girl Will thinks she is," he said hoarsely. "If she's in desperate trouble, she'll find her way out of it, somehow. Just as you would. You remind me of her, you know." He smiled, but Abby couldn't respond. She felt numb.

"After I broke my rib, I had time to think, lying in the wagon. I was almost relieved to be hurt," Matthew admitted. "I even talked myself into thinking Molly wouldn't want me to interfere. I imagined leaving your family, to look for her one last time, and losing you instead. What if I never saw you again?"

A strange queasiness settled in the pit of Abby's stomach. She shifted uneasily. She felt as if Matthew had cast another spell over her, dissolving her anger, making her forget all her questions. She quivered with a strange mixture of fear and excitement.

"I don't know what to do now," he said quietly. "I have no horse. I'm still too weak to travel on my own. But Will clearly wants me to go."

Abby finally found her voice. "Will's not in charge," she said calmly. "Even though he acts that way."

Matthew cupped Abby's chin in his palm and tipped her face up. She stared at his streaked, muddy face, hearing him from some dreamy place outside herself. "Your brother's right about one thing," he said softly. "I would like to kiss you."

He bent to touch her lips lightly, so quickly Abby was never sure, afterward, if she'd really felt the gentle brush of his mouth on her own. It was only later, remembering the scratch of his cheek, that she realized he'd lost the smooth, boyish skin he'd had in Independence. For now, she felt suspended somewhere, watching a thin girl in a dirty dress return his kiss. She looked down on her own face, splotched with tears and freckles. Was this the same girl whose mother taught her how to behave, who was stern about boys and men? This girl seemed to forget her lessons, ignored her brother's warnings entirely—in fact, she put her hands eagerly into Matthew's and smiled.

"What do you think you're doing?"

Uncle Joseph's harsh voice brought Abby back to the ground with a crash. Her heart plummeted to the soles of her moccasins as Matthew dropped her hands and stepped away.

Abby looked her uncle straight in the eye. Nothing, she promised herself silently, could destroy the way she felt this instant.

"Don't you have anything to say?" Uncle Joseph demanded. "My nephew comes back to camp with a fat lip, refusing to talk. Now I find you taking advantage of my niece—" His eyes danced from Matthew to Abby and back again, and his chin jutted forward, waggling his beard.

"I'm sorry about Will." Matthew sounded calm and self-assured, as if he'd gone to that same faraway place with Abby and come back restored. "That was a misunderstanding between us. As for Abigail"—he brushed her fingers lightly with his own, sending a shiver down her back—"I was kissing her. And I think she liked it."

"What kind of impertinent answer is that?" Uncle Joseph roared. When Matthew didn't answer, Uncle Joseph paced up and down in the long grass. "I should never have listened to the women. 'He'll be such a help,'" he mimicked in a high, falsetto voice. "They felt sorry for you. Poor boy, they thought. No mother or father, and *so* handsome. You think more about the ladies than your jobs with this company. We could have left you by the road anytime, have you thought of that?"

"I haven't forgotten your kindness," Matthew said. "I'm very grateful."

"Grateful!" Uncle Joseph pounded his open palm with a tight fist. "Nearly killing yourself at the ferry—

was that gratitude? Losing all the animals when you took watch? Hauling my niece up a cliff, and bashing Will in the mouth—you call that gratitude?"

Abby couldn't stand it any longer. "He didn't haul me up Chimney Rock, Uncle Joseph. I wanted to go. And Will started this fight. He's as much to blame as Matthew."

Uncle Joseph ignored her. "You listen to me, Reed. If you have designs on my niece, forget them. I'm standing in for her father, and I want you to know we don't approve of your kind. The sooner you leave, the better."

"Excuse me." Mother was suddenly right next to them, her approach masked by the sighing of the wind. Will stood behind her, pressing a cloth to his bleeding mouth.

Mary Parker pulled herself to her full height. "I don't know who's the cause of all this. But I heard what you said, and I'm afraid you're too hasty. You're not standing in for her father, Joseph. She's my daughter, and her behavior is my affair."

Uncle Joseph stepped back as if she'd slapped him, and stared, his eyes bulging.

"And as far as Matthew goes," Mother continued, "I think you've forgotten the agreement we made in Independence. You didn't want a hired man, did you? But I did. *I* took him on. Isn't that correct?" She looked from Uncle Joseph to Matthew. They both nodded. Abby was astonished. She'd always assumed, from the way her uncle behaved, that Matthew worked for him.

"Your part of the agreement," Mother continued, turning to Matthew, "was that you'd stay with me until we reached California. Isn't that correct?"

"Yes, ma'am."

Abby had never seen Matthew look so sheepish. She glanced at Will; he was hiding a smile behind his bloody handkerchief.

"That being so, you broke your part of the bargain when you chased after your sister at the ferry."

It was more a statement than a question, but Matthew answered, "That's right. And I apologize. But I always intended to come back."

Mother nodded. "I understand. Sarah Walker has explained your sister's difficulties. I want you to know that when the time comes, we'll do what we can to help you find her. But not until your rib is properly healed. Is that clear?"

"Yes, Mrs. Parker." Matthew's face was sober and taut.

The wind whistled through the dry grass. Abby glanced at her mother. She couldn't think when she'd ever heard her say so much at once. Uncle Joseph seemed stunned; he hadn't opened his mouth.

"What started all this?" Mother demanded, her eyes searching the group.

Uncle Joseph cleared his throat. "A misunderstanding," he said. "The boy took some liberties."

"What do you mean?" Mother asked.

"Matthew kissed me," Abby said clearly.

To Abby's surprise, Mother's eyes softened, and she

regarded her brother-in-law with disbelief. "That's the silliest thing I ever heard of," she said. "Can't two young people have a bit of privacy, without you barging in?"

Abby was astonished. Mother didn't mind. She held her breath, wondering what might happen next, but Uncle Joseph stomped off toward the wagons without a backward glance.

"Settle your differences, Will and Matthew," Mother ordered. "There's enough hardship as it is."

Matthew held out his hand to Will. "I think you already know I'm sorry."

Will nodded and took his hand quickly. "Shake," he said quietly. "Perhaps I spoke too hastily about Molly," he added.

Matthew shook his head. "No one knows what's happened to her," he said. "We're all arguing over someone we may never see." He grinned suddenly, poking Will in the ribs. "Smile," he teased.

Will obeyed, pulling his lips back in a grimace to reveal the bleeding gap in his lower jaw.

"You look like the trapper!" Abby exclaimed.

Will pulled the tooth from his pocket and thrust it at Matthew. "A souvenir," he said. To Abby's relief, they both laughed.

"Sometimes a fight clears the air," Mother said. "Go on back to the wagons now. The noon break is over."

Will and Matthew stumbled away together, pushing each other from side to side as though all their harsh words had been forgotten. When they were out of earshot, Abby said, "I didn't mean to cause trouble."

"I've seen it coming," Mother said dryly. "Matthew's had his eye on you the whole trip. Will and Joseph are like mother hens, trying to protect you. A kiss is all right, Abigail. But you be careful."

"Mother!"

Her mother's face softened, for an instant. "Don't worry. I trust you. Matthew's a nice young man. But you keep hold of yourselves." Mother paused, and small lines of worry caught the corners of her mouth. "Sometimes I wonder if we've forgotten who we are, out here with only the wind for company."

Abby heard the loneliness in her mother's voice, but she didn't know how to help. She felt as if the events of the last week—Matthew's accident, Suzy's death, Will's dark anger—had etched hairline cracks on the surface of her own heart. She threw herself into Mother's arms and burst into tears.

Her mother didn't resist. She held Abby tight and rubbed her back just below her shoulders. "Dear child," she said. "You've had to grow up all at once on this journey."

Abby's eyes strayed over the high peaks of the Wind River Mountains, but she hardly saw them. She was a little girl again, sheltered from the storms inside her by Mother's firm and wiry embrace.

July 15, 1850.

Dearest Caroline,

We're on the far side of the divide! We reached South Pass, the halfway point, on the 12th of July and stopped there to celebrate. We feasted on cooked game and pies made of dried apples. Then we had a dance, and I must admit I never sat down all night. Matthew's broken rib still pains him, but he took a few turns on the "dance floor" anyway. (Some of the men had set out a big piece of zinc for dancing.) Being the only women, Mother, Emma, Mrs. Walker, and I were much in demand, and my head was whirling when I went to bed.

We would never have found South Pass if Captain Foster hadn't read about it in Fremont's book. It's a wide, dry plain; not the way I imagined the Continental Divide, but definitely a place for my scrapbook. Looking to the east, I knew all the water flowed toward home. To the west, the streams rushed toward Pa. I tried to look both ways at once.

After South Pass, our company nearly split up, arguing over the route. Some men hoped to pass near Salt Lake to buy fresh food from the Mormons. But Mr. Grey argued in favor of Sublette's Cut-off, a shorter route, which avoids the desert at the Great Salt Lake. Mother surprised everyone by agreeing with him. (I guess she's in a hurry to see Pa.) In the end, only Mrs. Walker and her husband decided to go to Salt Lake. Mother wept when they parted. Friendships mean much more out here, so far from home.

*From the stream called the Big Sandy we traveled
fifty miles without water. We marched all night and day,
until we reached a steep precipice. The Green River
was coiled like a rope at the bottom. It took every one of
us to lower the oxen and wagons down the cliff without
an accident.*

*This may be the last letter I can send until we reach
the Yuba River. Remember I'm always your loving sister,*

Abigail

July 19. In the Bear River Valley.

Abby lowered her face to the clear water and drank
until she was full. Then she closed her eyes, held her
breath, and plunged her head into the river. She came
up spluttering and laughing. Water dripped onto her
shoulders and ran down inside her dress.

"Emma!" Abby called. "It's paradise!"

The river must have drowned Abby's voice, for
Emma sat motionless upstream, soaking her feet in a
deep pool, her eyes lost in the valley's enchantment.

Abby pulled up her skirts and waded into the water.
The cold current pushed at her shins and made V-
shaped rivulets around her ankles, soothing her tired
feet. She could never describe the Bear River in her

scrapbook. The river's deep song rolled around in her head at night, mingling with the plaintive tunes on Matthew's harmonica, but when she took up her pen to write about it, the words were dull and flat on the page.

Emma waved to her, and Abby struggled to shore. She climbed onto the bank and took a deep breath, filling her lungs with hot air. Mountains spread wide arms around the river bottoms, and afternoon shadows slid up and down the bluffs that formed skirts at their feet. Ducks wheeled above the marshes. No wonder the trapper loved it here.

Abby squeezed water from the hem of her skirt and ran to Emma. "Are you cooled off?"

Emma nodded. "Give me a hand." She stretched a gloved palm toward Abby. "It's hard to get up sometimes."

Abby steadied her aunt as she stepped carefully out of the river and pulled on her boots. Her belly was swollen beneath a thin layer of calico. Abby was so accustomed to the slow change in her aunt's figure that she sometimes forgot there was a baby underneath.

Timothy and Chester waited in the shade of a tree, nuzzling at the soft grass. They were a few miles ahead of their wagons. Emma had shocked Abby at the noon stop by suggesting they go hunting. When Abby stared at her aunt in disbelief, Emma had laughed. "Don't look so surprised!" she said. "I can shoot a gun. Besides," she reminded Abby, "you promised we'd go riding together sometime. Go on, tell Matthew we're taking the horses." She had ducked into her wagon and produced a rifle Abby had never seen. "Mother gave it to me when I left home," Emma explained. Then the two of them had set off quickly, careful that Uncle Joseph didn't see them leave.

Now the gun was propped against the tree beside the horses, and the rest of the family was nowhere in sight. Abby hefted the rifle, feeling the fine balance from its tip to its curly maple stock.

"Just like Pa's," Abby said. "A converted Kentucky rifle." She remembered when Pa removed the flint from his gun and substituted percussion caps. Everyone in town laughed at him, but soon they came into his store for the fittings. Pa had taught her to shoot; she wondered if she could do it without him.

"Come on, help me up," Emma said. "Let's find some ducks before the others catch up."

Abby set the gun down and wove her fingers together, making a basket of her hands. "Put your knee here," she said. Emma grabbed Chester's mane, rested her knee on Abby's hands and lunged upward. Abby strained beneath her aunt's weight as she hoisted her onto the horse.

"I'm on!" Emma cried, settling both legs primly on one side of the saddle.

Abby peered up at her aunt. "I don't understand how you can ride that way."

"My father said there's only way for a woman to ride a horse, although *you* certainly do it differently! Never mind. You know I'm careful."

All the urgency of the journey drained out through

Abby's legs into the billowing dust. I could stay here forever, she thought as they rode single-file away from the caravans toward the bluffs, where undulating folds of land flattened close to the river. When they reached a swath of wet, emerald marshland, a flock of geese rose and flew in confused circles above the water. "There's our supper!" Abby cried.

They tied their horses to some small trees and hurried to the edge of the bog. Emma took the leather bag from her shoulder and pulled out bullets, a powder horn, some caps, and scraps of cloth. They loaded the gun together, carefully ramming a bullet down the muzzle and holding it gingerly, as if it might explode in their faces.

"Can you shoot it?" Emma asked. "I'm afraid, with the baby."

Abby shrugged. "I guess so." She took the gun under her arm, pointing it toward the ground. Emma motioned for her to hide behind a rock while she crept forward toward the water.

Abby remembered how delicate Emma seemed when the trip began, how she wouldn't eat, and was constantly tired. Now she was dragging her swollen belly through the tall reeds, soiling her skirts. Wisps of hair fell from her thick coil. Abby marveled at the way the journey had changed everyone.

Emma pointed to a spot where the reeds were swaying gently. "Something's in there," she hissed. "I'll flush it out. Then you shoot."

Abby raised the gun to her shoulder and cocked the

first trigger. She sighted along the smooth barrel. The last time she hoisted Pa's gun more than a year ago, the recoil had thrown her back into his arms, and her shot went wild. This time, there was no one to catch her if she fell, but she was stronger now; her body was wiry and resilient from miles of walking. She dropped to one knee and shifted her weight until she felt balanced. The spongy ground soaked immediately through her skirt.

"Ready?" Emma whispered.

Abby swallowed hard. "I guess so."

Emma jumped to one side, clapped her hands, and shouted. The reeds burst with sound and movement as a flock of ducks exploded from the water, rending the air with frantic, throaty cries. Abby tried to spot one, then another, and finally aimed the muzzle into the blur of wings. She touched the trigger and swayed with the gun's recoil.

"Bravo!" Emma shouted as Abby caught her balance. "Did you hear the splash?"

Abby set the gun on a rock and ran to the edge of the marsh. Sodden ground gave way to pools of stagnant water. She covered her mouth with one hand. A duck floundered in the shallows.

"It's not dead," Abby moaned. She reached out to grab the bird. Its feathers opened like a fan, revealing a hole where the wing met the soft, rust-colored body.

She dragged the duck from the water and dropped it gently on the grass. Blood oozed over its dark chest. The bird struggled helplessly, hurling its head from side to side, and then, just as Abby was about to reach for her knife, it was still.

Abby's hands shook. "It's so beautiful," she said sadly. "What do you suppose it is?"

"Cinnamon teal." A strange, rough voice rang out behind them. Emma gasped, but Abby dropped the bird and took a step toward the trees. The trapper! When his lank, stooped form stepped out of the bushes, she ran toward him and put out her hands.

"You found us!" she cried.

"Abby!" Emma grabbed for her arm, but Abby pulled away. The trapper's hair had grown longer; the dirty strands trailed below his shoulders. His deerskin coat was torn and his hands were stained a deep brown.

"Pardon me, ma'am," the trapper said, tipping his hat to Emma. "Didn't mean to scare." He nodded toward Abby. His honey-colored eyes, the shape of almonds, flickered with amusement as he gestured toward the valley with a sweep of his arm.

"Welcome to my home," he said, taking in the green pleated hills, the distant wagon train, and the pine trees etched against a cobalt sky.

"I *thought* you must live here," Abby said. "I've been watching for you." She was aware of Emma moving behind her, but she wouldn't take her eyes off the trapper, for fear he might disappear.

"Watch where you point that thing!" the trapper shouted. Abby whirled around. Emma had picked up her gun; she stood with the muzzle wavering in the air.

"Emma, he won't hurt us!" Abby cried. "He's a friend."

The trapper took off his hat and stuck a finger through a round hole at the crown. "Been shot once already today," he said. "Lucky the customer weren't as good a shot as old Indian Trader here. May look fierce, but this one won't hurt a lady, he won't."

"I'm sorry," Emma whispered. "You frightened me." She lowered the gun but kept her feet braced and licked her lower lip. "We women have to be careful."

"Yes. There's some that aren't." The trapper winked at Abby.

Emma cleared her throat. "Come on, Abby. Let's go back. They'll miss us."

"Just a minute," Abby said. "Tell me, please—did you find her?"

"Don't know for sure it's who you want," the trapper said. "Couldn't get close enough to see if she matched the picture in here." He tapped his head. "She weren't too friendly." He whirled his hat around on his index finger and laughed.

Abby gasped. "Molly tried to shoot you?"

Emma looked from the trapper to Abby with astonishment. "Abby, what's going on? Did you send him looking for Molly?"

"This one's determined," the trapper said, pointing at Abby. "She's a match for the one ahead." He squinted and scratched his beard. "Don't know as anyone else could bring her out."

"Bring her out? Where is she?" Abby inched closer to the trapper and looked up into his face.

"Alone in a tent," he said. "Above Soda Springs. Won't let anyone near her. Folks say she's gone loco. From what you told me, I'd say she's the one."

Abby ran to Timothy, untied him, and scrambled onto his back. "I'm coming with you," she announced to the trapper. "How far is Soda Springs?"

"A few miles. We ride over that hill, we can save some time. I'll get my mule."

Emma tugged urgently at Abby's dress, as if she were a small child at her knee. "Abby, you can't go off alone with a strange man." She dropped her voice to a whisper. "He might do something to you. Maybe it's all a trap. How do you know it's really Molly?"

Abby watched the trapper slouch away, his hands dangling by his sides. His whole body was loose as a shank of rope, his legs bent wide, molded to the shape of his mule.

"He won't hurt me," Abby said. "And Molly's in serious trouble. Matthew's too far behind to do anything. How would you feel if you were all alone like Molly, with no one to help you? Please, ride back to the wagons. Tell them I'll wait at Soda Springs, no matter what."

"Abby, you're impossible!" Emma cried, wringing her hands. "What will I tell your mother?"

"She'll understand. She promised Matthew we'd help him." In fact, Abby didn't believe this for a minute.

Mother would be angry. And as for Uncle Joseph...
She was relieved when the trapper reappeared, riding
his mule.

"I'll take good care of this one," he said. "Don't you
worry. That girl up ahead ain't got much time. Take a
woman to reach her now. And it don't look like you're
the one to go," he added, pointing to Emma's belly.

Emma gasped. "Why, you certainly are rude—"

"That I am," he said lightly. "Been away from civilized people too long. Suits me fine. Come on, Indian
Trader. We got work to do."

Abby placed the duck across Emma's saddle. "Please,
take this back for supper. I'll be all right. I promise."

She kicked Timothy hard, and he jumped to a canter.
"Come on, boy!" she cried. "Go after that mule. We're
going to find Molly Reed, you and I. Won't that be
something?"

The pony whickered. Dust boiled around his legs as
they galloped out of the valley toward the bluffs.

July 19. Soda Springs.

For about an hour, Abby and Timothy kept a steady
pace just behind the trapper. The scrawny mule must
have known every hollow and stone on the bluffs, for
the trapper let the reins dangle as they picked their way
along the edge of the valley; his hands rested loosely on

his thighs. Occasionally, he swept an arm skyward toward a flock of pintails or jabbed a finger toward a ravine where Abby glimpsed a flash of white. Was it an
antelope's rump? A jackrabbit? Before she could be
sure, it disappeared in the green shadows.

The trail was rocky. When Timothy stumbled, the
trapper would turn casually. Just making sure I'm here,
Abby thought. She knew she looked very unladylike,
with her skirts bunched up and her legs wrapped tight
as the girth around the pony's belly, but she didn't care.

Abby turned and looked back. From the crest of this
bluff, she could see forward along the silver thread of
the river, but all the wagons were hidden from view.
She wondered what Matthew would think when Emma
told him where she'd gone. This was *his* search. Would
he ever forgive her? But after all, Abby reassured herself, it was only in the last few days that he'd even felt
like riding a horse again. If she'd gone back to the
wagons, she'd have wasted precious time—and who
knew how long the trapper would be willing to wait for
her? Abby clucked to Timothy. It was too late to worry
about it now.

The mule scrabbled over the top of a bony ridge.
Abby edged her pony up beside him and looked down
the steep hillside. A mountain stream had furrowed out
a little valley of its own before running across the wagon
trail to join the river. Choke cherries, mountain maple,
and scrawny pines clustered near the banks. At first,
the scene looked perfectly ordinary, until the trapper
pointed to a spot midway up the hill, where a large

crowd huddled close to the water.

"What are they doing?" Abby asked.

"Drinking soda," the trapper said. "Water boils like a kettle on the fire. Scoop out a cup, let it cool—you've got soda water."

Something else for her river scrapbook. Abby felt as if she'd been chewing wool all afternoon and was about to suggest a drink when she saw the isolated tent on the far bank, high above the brook. A flash of sunlight winked at them across the gorge.

"Look!" Abby cried. "Is that Molly?"

The trapper shrugged. "Girl gives herself away, flashing a gun like that." He pulled his own heavy rifle from its strap on his saddlebags and hoisted it up in front of him. "No shine on this mountain gun," he said proudly, stroking the dark wood where it joined the iron muzzle.

"There's no need for anyone to shoot, is there?" Abby asked nervously.

"Don't know," the trapper said. "She told folks three days ago she ain't going nowhere. Most folks don't care. 'She wants to die out here alone, that's her affair,' says one." The trapper stabbed his chest. "*This* one says: That ain't right."

Abby peered into his face, stern with wrinkles from the sun. Concern flickered in his eyes. "Lots of people would just abandon her," said Abby, "the way they did the Walkers. I believe you're more civilized than they are."

The trapper kicked his mule, ignoring her comments, and Abby followed him off the ledge. Even though he appeared tough and crusty, she guessed he was soft as a baby underneath.

The horses picked their way down the hill. When they reached the bottom, the trapper drew up on his mule and gestured toward a line of Douglas fir, cutting jagged outlines against the sky. "Head up that way, we can come down on her from behind," he explained. "Take her by surprise."

Abby didn't ask what they would do if Molly took a shot at them. For the first time in weeks, she wished for a sunbonnet—anything to cover the red beacon of her hair.

"Look there." The trapper flicked his elbow in the direction of the tent. Something white floated in the tent's opening and disappeared. Abby suddenly remembered the small triangular face in Matthew's daguerreotype. It was hard to match the girl in that picture, her eyes glistening with life, with the desperate person on the far side of the stream.

The hill grew steep. Timothy's breath came in short, hard bursts; Abby panted and leaned forward over his shoulders to help him climb. When they reached the tree line, they turned and plunged down the ridge to the stream. Abby reversed her weight, laced her fingers through Timothy's mane, and arched back toward his rump. She settled her weight over Timothy's hind legs and let her spine ride back and forth as he slid over the gravel.

The trapper glanced back and gave her an approving nod. "Where'd Indian Trader learn to ride?" he asked.

"Pa taught me," Abby said, wondering if she'd end up speaking in choppy sentences like the trapper before the day was through. "I sometimes wonder if he'll ever see me ride again."

"He got any sense, he'll be there when Indian Trader comes along," said the trapper.

Abby smiled, hoping he was right. Lately, she'd avoided thinking about Pa. It would be too awful if they'd made this trip for nothing.

When the slope leveled off, the trapper called out, "Your pony's worth gold. Watch the Diggers. They'd steal him while you sleep."

"The Diggers?"

"Desert Indians. Strange people. Move like shadows, live like desert rats. Fagh!" The trapper edged ahead of Abby and hunched his shoulders, and Abby guessed he was through with talk for a while.

They rode in silence across the stream, followed a zigzag course over the hill, and circled up behind the tent, where the trapper hissed, "Off here."

Abby climbed down and dropped the reins over Timothy's neck. He stood still when the reins touched the ground; Pa had taught him that. The trapper nodded with approval. "Want a gun?" he asked.

Abby shook her head. "She has to trust me." She waited for the trapper to tell her what to do, but he was silent. Her mouth felt dry, and her hands were clammy, in spite of the heat. On an impulse, she grabbed the trapper's hand and wrung it hard. "Goodbye. Wish me luck." She drew her fingers back quickly, feeling the deep grooves and calluses on his palm.

"Yep. Good luck, Indian Trader," he said. "She talks to you, bring her here. If she won't come, don't linger."

Abby nodded. "I'll be all right." She didn't believe it. Her knees felt wobbly. She rubbed the pony's head and kissed him between the eyes. If only she could hide beneath his round belly and wait for Matthew!

She stepped out into the sunlight and crept down the hill in a half-crouch, darting from one pile of rocks to the next, and stopped in a tangle of currant bushes, about fifty feet from the tent. Someone had stripped the shrubs clean. Did Molly come out of the tent at night to forage for food? She must feel like a wild animal. Abby studied the space between herself and the tent. There was no shelter there; from now on, she'd be out in the open. The dingy canvas flapped gently in the hot breeze.

Abby took one cautious step forward and froze as a woman's clear voice sounded right behind her.

"Stop where you are. Right there. Or I'll shoot you."

Abby turned around slowly and bit her lip. A young woman scrambled out of the bushes. She held a gun stiffly in front of her.

The woman looked weak. For an instant, Abby thought she could knock her down. Then she remembered the hole in the trapper's hat. Better to keep things steady and calm. "You're Molly, aren't you? I'm a friend. Please put the gun down. I won't hurt you."

The young woman's eyes narrowed with suspicion. She gripped the rifle tightly across her chest. "Who told you my name? Did Judson send you up here? Tell him I'm finished with his tricks. Go away, and I won't shoot you. Go on."

In spite of her fear, Abby almost laughed. The dancing, fierce light in this woman's eyes was so like Matthew's. Abby controlled her voice when she spoke again. "I'm a friend of your brother, Matthew. He'll be here soon. If you put the gun down, I can take you to him. I have a horse."

Molly wavered. Her hands shook violently, and her body swayed a little. She looked ravenous; her arms were like sticks, and her dress hung from her shoulders. Piles of black curls were matted close to her scalp.

"It's a trick," Molly whispered. "Judson told you about my brother."

"No," Abby insisted. "I promise. Matthew's been with us for months now. He's been searching everywhere for you."

Suddenly Molly straightened. "Liar!" she shrilled. "If he's so eager to find me, why isn't he here now? I know my brother. He wouldn't send some puny red-haired *girl* after me! He'd come himself. He's no coward. Now get out of here. Leave!" She spit the words in Abby's face and raised the gun's muzzle until it poked her in the belly.

Abby flinched and stared at Molly in disbelief. Waves of rage boiled up inside her. "Stay here, then!" Abby shrieked, shaking her fist. "Kill yourself! You're just as stupid and stubborn as the rest of your family. Your father *died*, trying to protect you. Matthew almost drowned, swimming after you. Well, I can see you're not worth it."

Abby shook with fury. This foolish girl, with her gun and her wild, lost eyes, had caused nothing but trouble. Let her die.

"When my uncle catches me," Abby said, her teeth clenched tight as her fists, "he'll take my horse away. Mother will never trust me again. I'll lose Matthew as a friend. You're a stupid fool."

Abby turned on her heel, ignoring the gun. "Go ahead. Starve to death!" she cried over her shoulder. "But don't expect me to wait around. I'm through watching your family behave like imbeciles!"

Tears streamed down Abby's face. She knew she ought to worry about a bullet searing her spine, but anger pushed her forward.

"Wait!" Molly called in a shaken voice. "Please don't leave."

Abby stopped, but kept her back turned. "Drop the gun," she demanded. When she heard the clang of metal on stone she pivoted slowly, half expecting a trick. But Molly was swaying; she toppled sideways. Abby ran and caught her just before she hit the ground. They were both crying now; Molly turned her face against Abby's dress and sobbed, her body arching with each wrenching cry.

"Is it true, what you said?" she gasped. "My father's dead?"

Abby stroked Molly's tangled hair, ashamed of her outburst. "I'm sorry. I didn't mean to tell you that way.

Matthew can explain everything when he comes."

Molly turned her head and looked up into Abby's face. Her body gave off the sweet, slightly sickening odor of someone who's stopped eating.

"You had no choice," Molly whispered. "I'd lost my senses."

Abby managed a weak smile. "Mother always said my temper would be the end of me. I think it saved my life today." She wiped her face with the back of her hand. "Do you think you can walk? My pony's up on the hill."

Molly pulled herself to her knees and looked deep into Abby's eyes. Her voice was thin. "I can walk. But how can I face anyone? I'm too ashamed to see Matthew. I ran away, and wasn't married. Then, when I wouldn't behave like a wife, Judson beat me." Her eyes grew wild again and Abby shuddered. She didn't want to imagine what Molly's journey had been like.

"There was a woman in our caravan. Sarah Walker," Molly continued. "She looked out for me. But our company abandoned her. And I was left alone."

"She traveled with us for a ways," Abby said. "She told us all about you. But she's gone to Salt Lake."

Molly just stared, as if she was too numb to take anything in. She spoke in a flat, dull monotone. "After the Walkers were gone, Judson started in on me again. Said if I wouldn't act like a wife, he'd sell me in the mines." She gulped, shivering. "I wouldn't give in. I wouldn't." Molly crossed her arms across her chest, as if still protecting herself. "And then, one night, I heard him talking to the other men. He was offering me to the highest bidder.... I stole his gun and ran away. I shot at him twice, when he tried to come after me; I never slept—"

"Hush, hush," Abby said. Her stomach crawled, listening. "Don't worry. It's all over now."

"But don't you see!" Molly cried. "Everyone will think I'm a—" She gulped, unable to say the word.

"Not Matthew," Abby said. "He knows you're a good person."

Molly wiped her eyes. "I hope so," she said brokenly. She stood up and put a hand on Abby's shoulder to steady herself. "I'm ready to go," she said. "I just had to tell someone. Please believe me, I'm not what I seem."

"I believe you," Abby said, and she did. But she wondered what the rest of her family would say.

They walked slowly up the hill. Molly nearly fell twice and stopped often to catch her breath. After each rest, Abby renewed her grip on Molly's waist and pulled her forward. "Has Judson Hall left the springs?" Abby asked.

"I guess," Molly said. "The last I saw him was three days ago. But I kept having nightmares about him. I'd doze off and dream he was after me again. It was horrible." Molly stared at Abby, as if she were just now waking up. "Who are you, anyway? You never told me your name!"

Abby laughed. "You didn't give me a chance. I'm Abby Parker. Matthew's been traveling with my family."

"I see." But Molly stared quizzically at Abby, as if she didn't understand at all. "Why did you come after me, and not Matthew?"

As simply as she could, Abby explained about Matthew's accident and her meetings with the trapper. Molly nodded vaguely, as if she only heard half of what Abby said. When they heard hoofbeats, Molly gripped Abby's arm in fright and then stared at the trapper, who was approaching with Timothy.

"Oh, I've been such a fool!" she wailed. "That's the man I tried to *shoot* this morning!" She buried her face in her hands, then faced the trapper with streaming eyes. "Please forgive me. I never dreamed I'd hit you—I only meant to scare you away."

The trapper touched his hat. "Glad you missed." He pointed down the hill toward the spring. "You got more company now." Abby recognized Matthew's tall figure seated on Chester. As the red horse scrambled up the rocky slope, Matthew whirled his hat over his head and shouted; Abby couldn't make out his words.

"Matt!" Molly whimpered, and began to run, weaving precariously down the slope they had just climbed.

"Molly, be careful!" Abby started after her, but the trapper grabbed her shoulder.

"Let them be, Indian Trader. She's got strength to do what she wants."

Abby bounced from one foot to the other, nearly dancing with frustration and impatience.

The trapper laughed. "She pull a gun?"

"She ambushed me!" Abby exclaimed, keeping her eyes fixed on Molly and Matthew. "I yelled at her. It's a wonder she didn't shoot *me!*"

"You did well," the trapper said as they watched Matthew leap from Chester's back into Molly's tight embrace.

Tears stung Abby's eyes. "*You're* the one who brought them together," she insisted, brushing the trapper's hand with her fingers. "Please, don't go away. I'll be right back."

She skipped down the hill, clutching her skirts above the knee. Halfway down, she slowed to a walk. Would she be in the way? But when Matthew caught sight of her, his face shone above the dark ring of his sister's curls.

"Abby!" he cried, as she ran to him. "Thank God. You found her!"

Relief flooded through Abby. Matthew wasn't angry. She stepped into his beckoning arm and let herself fall against him. Molly huddled close to them both. All three faces were wet with tears.

"Don't thank me," Abby said at last, her voice muffled against Matthew's shoulder. "Thank the trapper."

Molly pulled away and groaned. "I tried to kill that man this morning. Can you ever forgive me, Matt? For that, and everything else?"

Matthew laughed. "Of course." He kissed Molly.

His sister flinched and pulled away. "Matthew, you don't know," she whispered. "It wasn't what you think—"

He put a finger to her lips. "No. Whatever happened is done now. It wasn't your fault." He tipped Abby's

head toward him and looked into her eyes. "You'll have
to explain. How did the trapper know about Molly?
Were you plotting behind my back?"

Abby nodded. "I didn't mean to, but when you were
hurt, at the ferry, I met the trapper. He said he was
going this way—I asked him to keep an eye out for
Molly. And I *did* show him the daguerreotype," she admitted.

"So I do have you to thank," Matthew said. He
looked up the hill. "Where's the trapper now?"

Abby turned and squinted into the sun. Timothy
stood alone on the crest of the hill, waiting obediently
with his reins dangling. "He was right there," she said
suddenly. "He can't have gone. I didn't thank him! I
wanted to cook the duck for his dinner." Abby ran up
the hill a little way and scanned the woods, frantically
searching for some sign of the mule and its lanky rider.
But the rocky hillside was barren and empty.

"I didn't say goodbye!" Abby wailed. "I'll never see
him again!"

Matthew put both hands on her shoulders and turned
her around. "Don't fret," he said. "He might come
back."

Abby knew he wouldn't. The trapper hated crowds.
And he wouldn't want her to thank him in front of
everyone. He was too proud. He'd rather slip away un-
noticed.

"Abby, are you ready?" Matthew asked. "We've got
some explaining to do this time. We'd better go to your
family."

Abby slipped her hand through Molly's arm and grabbed Matthew's wrist. "*Your* family, too," she said, and blushed to the roots of her hair.

August 2, 1850. "City of Rocks."

Dearest Caroline,
Even though we can't mail letters until we reach Sutter's Fort in California, I thought I would go on writing to you. We're camped in the strangest place, where there are huge pink rocks the size and shape of buildings. People have given them names like "The Courthouse" or "The Hotel." It's very crowded now. There's hardly room to stretch out a piece of canvas at night.

I found Matthew's sister, Molly, last week. It was a happy reunion for Matthew, but she's causing lots of problems. Will says Molly's not fit company for our family. Mother says we can't judge what was done to Molly against her will. Molly says she's done nothing to be ashamed of, except for running away in the first place.

I was in terrible trouble myself for a few days. Mother was appalled to think I'd gone off with a strange man to find Molly. But she's forgotten all about it now, because Captain Foster is very sick. Mother is doctoring him with medicines from her little box, but nothing seems to help. She calls his sickness "mountain fever." Uncle Joseph says the company will fall apart if the captain dies.

August 6.

We're in the Valley of One Thousand Springs. Mother thought the hot springs and the cold, fresh water would help the captain, but he died this morning, with Mother by his side. She never worries about getting sick herself. What would we do if she was ill?

Last night I almost agreed with Mr. Grey that we've had nothing but trouble since Molly came. Soon after the City of Rocks, we came to a steep descent. Mother's wagon broke loose from the ropes and was smashed to bits two thousand feet below. One of the oxen was killed, and all my things were scattered across the trail. I managed to save my river scrapbook, my letters to you, and a dress. Everything else was ground into the sand.

This is our last stop before the Humboldt River. Matthew is cooking rancid bacon in a boiling hot spring. I can't eat anything. I keep thinking about the captain's grave, just beside the road. It's so lonesome here, with the craggy mountains and the wolves howling.

Until I can write again, I'm always your loving sister,
Abigail

August 26. At the Humboldt Sink.

Abby pulled the strings of Mother's old sunbonnet tight beneath her chin. After days of pulsing heat, she'd finally agreed to wear it. Everything was hot to the touch; Pa's watch burned a fiery circle against her throat and the baked ground throbbed through the soles of her moccasins.

How long had they traveled beside the Humboldt River? Three weeks? Four? She'd lost track of time and had long since ranked this river at the bottom of her collection. It was a gray, wet snake, winding through a barren plain. It slowed the caravans to its own sluggish pace and forced them into constant detours around wet, boggy banks. The water tasted more and more salty as it crawled to its ending in a swamp.

Abby's eyes burned. She lifted them skyward, hoping for fresh, clean air above, but the cobalt bowl reflected heat back to the ground. Usually they slept after the noon stop, waiting for the sky to break open in the evening, releasing the earth's warmth. When the desolate hills stood like dark mounds on the horizon, they would yoke the oxen and trudge westward under the stars. But today, Uncle Joseph rounded everyone up after the noon meal and pushed them forward.

Abby wondered how long their caravan would hold together. Since the Valley of One Thousand Springs, the men had grudgingly accepted Uncle Joseph as their leader, but his short temper caused complaints. The strain of marching at night and sleeping by day took its toll; all their spirits were honed to a thin edge. In the last week, people and animals began to peel away like layers of an onion, until there were only six wagons left.

"Ho! Abigail!"

Four oxen pulled up beside her, their legs churning the baked earth to a fine powder. Abby recognized Will's stocky form walking beside them, but his face was a stranger's. A thin sheen of dust blurred his features and covered his clothes. "Ugly, isn't it?" he said.

"Horrible." Abby's kerchief muffled her voice. "Are we near the Sink?"

"Over there." Will's voice was thick and rasping. He pointed north, where the leaden river became a tangle of wet tracks, crawling toward a distant swamp. Then he flicked his whip idly over the near ox.

"Will, don't!" Abby cried. "They can hardly walk."

"They have to remember I'm here," Will said. "Otherwise they'll die on their feet."

Abby knew he was right. Dead carcasses strewn beside the trail reminded them of all the poor creatures who had already succumbed to the numbing monotony of the journey.

"Where's Molly?" Abby asked.

"In the wagon," Will said.

"No wonder the oxen are dragging!"

Will shrugged. "Try telling that to Mother. She's the one who said it was Molly's turn to rest."

Abby wished her brother would stop complaining about Molly, but she was too tired to protest. She squinted at the dry sea of prickly pear and sagebrush. All those long, itchy Sundays in church, when she'd sat idly wondering what hell was like—now she knew.

"Why are we traveling in this heat?" Abby asked crossly. "What's wrong with Uncle Joseph, anyway?"

"It's because of Mr. Grey. He wants to leave our family behind. He's talking about snow in the mountains."

"Snow?" Abby coughed. It seemed a joke, to think of snow now.

"Mr. Grey insisted we reach the Sink before dark," Will continued. "He thought Uncle Joseph would lag behind, to let Emma rest. But of course Emma said she'd walk like everyone else."

"Why doesn't Mr. Grey leave, like the others did?" Abby asked.

Will snorted. "Can't you guess? He's afraid of the Diggers."

Abby didn't blame him. Everyone hated the Diggers. They made life miserable, just as the trapper had warned. Yesterday, they stripped a man from the next company, tied him in his own clothes, and stole his mule. A few days ago, two Indians snatched a pan of hot cornmeal mush from Emma's hands. Day or night, no one slept soundly, since the Indians were brazen enough to steal things in broad daylight.

"He's afraid, but he'd let us face them alone?" Abby felt anxious, knowing this short, bristly man was plotting against her family. "Will, we can't let him do that. How can we stop him?"

"I don't know. He stirs everything up. That's why all

the good men took off on their own. They couldn't stand him anymore."

Abby tried to swallow, but her throat was too swollen. "I wish we'd stayed at One Thousand Springs," she whined.

"Don't remind me," Will snapped.

Memories of deep pools full of cold, clear liquid swirled in Abby's head. "Will, I need a drink." She staggered and leaned on her brother.

Will propped her up and stopped the oxen. "Pull yourself together," he said harshly.

"What's wrong?" Molly's head popped out from inside the wagon. Her black curls were matted from sleep; her face gleamed like a white heart in the burnished light.

"If you hadn't been asleep, maybe you'd know what's wrong," Will snapped.

Molly looked ashamed; she climbed quickly over the wheel and dropped to the ground. "Can I help?" she asked.

"Get me the flask," Will ordered, turning his back on her.

Abby swayed and lurched toward the wagon. Will grabbed the flask from Molly and shoved it into Abby's hands. "Here, take a sip. But only a little."

The tepid water soothed Abby's throat, but her head was swimming. Black dots wove slow circles across her vision. She closed her eyes and sank slowly into a deep pool.

When she came to, her arms were akimbo; someone was dragging her across the hot sand into the shade of some spindly trees. She tried to focus. Her head was floating. Will's face slowly took on distinct features; then Molly's gray eyes came out of the mist.

"Did I faint?" Abby whispered.

Will nodded.

Molly squeezed Abby's hand. "I'm sorry—you should have had a turn in the wagon. I didn't mean to fall asleep."

Abby felt as if her head might float away from her body. She was relieved when she heard Mother's brisk voice saying, "Let me see, please," and felt a cool hand skim her cheek.

"She's burning up," Mother said. "Will, hand me the flask." She pulled off her kerchief, wet it, and swabbed Abby's forehead before holding the flask to her lips. Abby drank greedily and then obeyed numbly when Mother pulled her to standing and said, "Come, Abigail. We'll walk to the swamp, and you can cool off there."

The pungent smell of dead animals made Abby queasy. She took Mother's arm as they approached the enormous meadow full of wet, trampled grass. Crowds of emigrants had scattered across the slough like geese, while oxen, horses, and mules had plunged their scrawny necks deep into the lush feed.

"The last stop for grass before the desert," Mother said. "We'll cut hay here tomorrow."

Abby took a tighter grip on Mother's arm, feeling the tightness of dry skin over bone. Mother's chest and eyes were sunken; gray hair circled her temples, and her

dress hung limp at the waist. Abby ran her fingers ten-
tatively over her own face and wished for their mirror,
broken when the wagon was smashed.

"Mother, you're so thin. Am I?" Abby asked.

Mother glanced at her. "We're both skinny," she admitted. "Now what's this? Are the men fighting again?"

A small crowd clustered near the lead wagon. Angry
voices snapped in the twilight, and Abby recognized
Mr. Grey's high-pitched whine.

"You told us what to do long enough!" he yelled.
"Now we make our own decisions!"

Uncle Joseph's face was blurred in the dusk, but
Abby knew from his stance—chin thrust out, arms stiff
at his sides—that rage was seething just below the surface. "Couldn't we talk about this in the morning?"

Mr. Grey strutted in front of him. "I got news for
you, Parker. We ain't going to be here in the morning.
The rest of us, even Frank Watson, we've discussed it.
We're going to the Carson River tonight."

Frank Watson? Abby couldn't believe he'd join with
Herbert Grey.

"I assume you'll make amends for your share of the
expenses," Uncle Joseph said calmly.

"Beg pardon." Mr. Grey's tone grew oily. "Seems to
me you're the one needs to make a payment. Didn't
you add two strangers to the company?"

Abby's stomach quivered. Where was Matthew? She
searched the circle and finally caught sight of him
standing, tall and quiet, just behind her uncle, with
Molly beside him.

"Good luck," Uncle Joseph said. "Your animals will certainly die if you don't recruit them here."

"You won't force me over Truckee Pass," Grey said. "The Donners ended up cannibals there, you know. Although I don't suppose that's any worse than what some members of your party have done." He leered at Molly.

The air crackled with tension. "Just what do you mean?" Molly darted into the circle, tossing her black curls. "I guess you've all decided I'm a bad woman. Mary Parker's the only one who asked me what really happened. She knows I just made one mistake." She took a step closer to Mr. Grey until her eyes were level with his. "I ran away with a man like you. Someone who hates women. And this is what you both deserve."

Molly drew back her arm and swung it, full force, at Mr. Grey, slapping him with a sharp whack. He recoiled and grunted, pressing a hand to his cheek. Scattered jeers and applause broke out around them.

Abby searched for Will in the crowd and was surprised to see him staring at Molly with a mixture of stunned approval and embarrassment.

"Hey, Grey! You gonna let a woman get away with that?" Angry muttering rose from the crowd like bees swarming. Abby's hands were wet; sweat trickled down inside her collar. Her family wouldn't have a chance if this turned into an ugly brawl.

"Excuse me." Mother's clear voice cut through the twilight. The swarthy, dark shadows of the men dwarfed her tiny figure, but she didn't seem to notice.

"Mr. Grey, you owe this lady an apology. She did

right to hit you. I was tempted myself."

Mr. Grey flinched and took a step backward. Will and Matthew both laughed, and Abby wondered for a moment if Molly might have brought everyone back together without realizing it, uniting them against Mr. Grey.

"Molly's done nothing to be ashamed of," Mother continued. "It's the men she was with who ought to be whipped for lack of decency. I believe you owe all the women here an apology, for the way you talk."

Mr. Grey's shifty eyes scanned the crowd for support. No one said a word. They seemed spellbound by this small woman with the neat coil of hair, who spoke to them like children.

"Beg pardon, ma'am," Mr. Grey muttered at last. "Now, could we get on with the business at hand?"

"Fine," Mother said briskly. "It's time to put it to a vote, isn't it, Joseph?"

Uncle Joseph looked startled. Abby grinned. She remembered Pa saying once, "It's your mother runs this family. Don't ever doubt it. I just come along to see what happens."

"Right," Uncle Joseph said, recovering his voice. "All in favor of the Truckee route, raise your hands high. Abigail, will you count please?"

Abby stepped into the circle. Molly, one; Matthew, two; Will, Mother, Uncle Joseph: three, four, five. She raised her own hand up above her head. Six.

"Over here, Abby," Emma called. Abby counted her aunt and watched, with relief, as Frank Watson's arm slowly lifted from the shoulder.

"That's eight, Uncle Joseph."

Herbert Grey began to shout. "Wait a minute! Who said anything about women voting?"

"They've as much right as you," Uncle Joseph said steadily. "Maybe more."

Abby smiled gratefully at her uncle, but he kept his eyes fixed on Herbert Grey. "Count your men now," he said. "Those who come with me will arrive safely at Sutter's Fort before snow falls, God willing."

"You wish." Mr. Grey paced inside the circle. "All right, boys, who's coming with me tonight? With a share of my profits to boot, once we rake it from the stream—and no *women* to slow us down?"

The rest of the men raised their hands sheepishly, avoiding the Parkers with their eyes. There were only five, counting Mr. Grey.

The group separated into two uneasy clumps, and an irrevocable silence crept over the campground. The lonely darkness fell quickly, as it did every night in the desert. The Parkers made their fire, ate some tough sage hens Matthew had shot, and grazed their animals.

Before she went to bed, Abby checked to make sure Timothy's rope was tight on his picket line. "Keep an eye on the pony, Will," she begged. He waved, and Abby curled up on the hard ground, pulling a tattered quilt around her. Just before she dozed into sleep, Molly knelt beside her and whispered, "Abby, I'm so ashamed. I've brought nothing but trouble."

Abby started and sat up quickly, finding Molly's eyes

in the dark. "That's not true," she said softly, and smiled. "You should have seen some of the things I did before we found you."

"Really?" Molly inched closer. "Will you tell me some time?"

Abby nodded. "Tomorrow. Here, get under the quilt with me."

Molly huddled beside her and whispered, "Your brother will never like me, now I've made such a fool of myself."

Abby giggled. "I think it's the opposite. You should have seen his face when you hit Mr. Grey. He likes you, he just doesn't know it yet." Abby hesitated. "Molly, do you like Will?"

"A little," Molly admitted. "But I don't dare think about it. I made such a big mistake with Judson."

"Will's okay," Abby said in a low voice. "He's just— well, stubborn, that's all. Before we found you, he decided you were bad. Now he sees you're not, but he can't admit it. Don't worry. He'll change."

They both laughed. Pulling the quilt over their heads, they continued whispering until the air grew cool and they could fall into a fitful sleep.

Sometime in the dead of night, Abby woke with a start. Wheels creaked past; Mr. Grey's party was leaving. Will and Uncle Joseph watched them go in silence. After all these months together, there were no farewells. The desert had consumed their great caravan.

Abby slept again and woke at dawn, already drenched in sweat. She stood up and tried to smooth her rumpled dress. Molly, Matthew, and Emma were still asleep. Mother, Uncle Joseph, and Will stood by the cold fire in dejected silence.

Abby ran to them. "What's wrong?" she demanded.

"Two oxen are missing," Will said. "I don't know how it happened; I never slept. But Mr. Grey drove his wagons between me and the animals when he left."

"He stole them," Abby said. No one disagreed. "Can we catch him?"

Uncle Joseph shook his head. "They've got six hours on us. Before two days are out, the oxen will die. There's nothing to do. We'll have to leave one wagon here."

What would happen to them now? They stood in stupefied silence, benumbed by the sun and their predicament. Heat rose, shimmering, over the swamp, a reminder of the desert to come.

September 2. Approaching the Truckee River.

"Up! Hup there! Gee up! Move, you blasted things! Come on up now!"

The long bullwhip snapped and whined outside the straining wagon, curling around Uncle Joseph's harsh voice. Emma squeezed Abby's fingers in the dark. "Better get out. We're too heavy. I'll be all right."

Emma's breathing quickened, and Abby knew the pains had come again. Of all nights for Mother to be gone, she thought. And Molly, too—what was Uncle Joseph thinking, sending them ahead for water? Please, please, she whispered to no one in particular, let us reach Mother before the baby comes.

She jumped over the churning wheel and fell into the deep sand. It was still dark; the sun was lost somewhere below the cradle of the desert, lurking under the vast bowl that threatened to eat them alive. For a moment, she couldn't see anything beyond the heaving legs of the oxen; then a cloud sailed past the moon, lighting the sand like snow and giving form to the shadowy figures struggling with the animals.

"Abby?" Matthew's voice rang out from the back of the wagon. "Can you help? We're mired again."

Abby slogged toward him. The fine silver grit filled her moccasins and sparkled like ice crystals in the moonlight.

Emma moaned inside the wagon, a deep, throaty sound that cleaved the darkness and threw Uncle Joseph into a frenzy of shouting. He cursed the night, the wretched oxen, the sand, and God.

Abby stumbled toward Frank and Matthew. Their faces were gaunt in the moonlight; sweat streaked their torn shirts. The three of them threw their weight against the wagon. It resisted like a mule; it balked, shuddered, and inched forward, then lurched backward, tossing Abby to the ground.

She fell flat, pulled herself up to her knees, and

caught her breath. Everything seemed hopeless. If she didn't have a drink soon, she'd shrivel up inside. But all the casks were empty.

"Need a boost?" Matthew cupped a hand under her elbow and hoisted her to standing just as Uncle Joseph appeared from the front of the wagon. His hair stood on end and his body nearly danced with rage. The sight of Matthew's hand on Abby's arm seemed to light a torch inside him.

"My God, Abigail!" he screamed. "What's the matter with you? Can't you see we're desperate? Every time I turn around, you're mooning at the boy. Emma could die, and you'd still flaunt your feelings. Well, I'll teach you two to keep your distance."

Abby was too afraid to be angry. Uncle Joseph's eyes were wild; he raised his hands menacingly above his head. "Don't!" Abby screamed. Matthew stepped in front of her as Emma's ghostly face appeared at the rear of the wagon.

"Joseph! What are you doing?"

Uncle Joseph whirled to face his wife, and for a horrible moment Abby thought he would beat Emma instead. But he lowered his arms and spat out his words in a harsh whisper. "You stay out of this, Emma. It doesn't concern you."

"Of course it concerns me, Joseph Parker. You just said I might die. Well, I have news for you. I don't intend to die, I intend to have a baby. If you'll stop screaming at everyone, perhaps we could move the wagon." Uncle Joseph's arms dropped to his sides, but he continued to glare at his wife. Emma's not afraid, Abby thought. How does she know he won't hurt her?

"And don't order me about," Emma was saying, looking down at him with a strange mixture of scorn and affection. "I'm not your serving maid, and neither is Abby. If you lay a hand on her, I'll never speak to you again. I mean that."

In the terrible, tense silence that followed, Abby heard the oxen groan and then a sharp hiss—the quick intake of breath that accompanied Emma's pains.

Abby skirted her uncle as if he were carrion. He still looked like a snake, poised for a strike. But Abby felt immune. She closed her hands over Emma's white knuckles.

"Emma." Abby was proud of the control in her voice. "Shall we lighten the wagon?"

"All right. I'll get out." Emma stepped down, her movements ponderous and awkward, and laughed as the men backed away from her. "Don't worry," she said. "It won't fall out in your laps." She caught her breath, swayed a little, then stood straight again.

The tension slowly ebbed as they piled things on the ground: their last bag of flour, filled with mealybugs; Emma's rocker; two small trunks that held what was left of their clothing; a couple of shovels. Matthew and Frank leaned their shoulders hard against the wagon box. Will and Uncle Joseph lurched to the oxen again, and soon their voices rang out, pleading with the animals to try one last time. Abby threw herself against the wagon and felt the wheels shift and then inch forward.

The oxen floundered out of the belly-deep sand onto firmer ground.

When the wagon was moving steadily, Will halted the oxen so they could reload. "I'm getting back in," Emma whispered to Abby. "You walk, if you can. We'll move faster that way. I'll be all right now."

"Are you sure?" Abby asked. She had an idea. Reaching into her dress, she pulled out her watch, slipped it over her head, and placed it in Emma's hand. "Keep this," she said, remembering something her mother had said to Caroline when Moses was born. "You can keep track of the pains."

Emma nodded and hoisted herself back into the wagon. She's having a baby, Abby thought, and neither one of us knows the first thing about it. She swallowed the tiny surge of panic that clutched her dry throat like a hand, and fell into a slow, labored pace behind the wagon.

Clouds swallowed the moon, and Abby stopped a minute. Did they load the chair? She thought of shovels going back in; flour, clothes—no, surely her uncle, fierce in his rage, had left the chair behind. But how else would Emma rock the baby? Abby whirled around, tripping in the heavy sand, and ran. Soon the moon reappeared, dropping a pool of light around the rocker.

Abby untied her apron and looped it through the rungs. Taking one end of the sash in each hand, she turned the chair's seat to the east and began to pull it forward. The rocker slid over the sand like sleigh runners on snow.

The loneliness of the desert enveloped her. The creak of the wagon, the prickling, mournful howl of a coyote, the snap of a whip—all were muffled, as if heard under water. Water. Abby sighed. No matter how she tried to control her thoughts, they always circled back to that word, to the memory of sweet liquid rolling over her tongue.

Abby held her breath. Something moved in the shadows ahead. A coyote? Frank told her you could stare them down, but she didn't want to try. Her heart raced. Digger Indians—could they live here, in this horrible place with no water? Abby took a few steps forward, and jumped when Matthew called her name.

"Matthew, you frightened me." Abby laughed with relief and hurried toward him. "I thought you were an animal—or an Indian." She peered into his shadowy face. "Why are you waiting for me? Didn't you hear what my uncle said? He doesn't want us together."

"I heard him." Matthew's voice was strained. "I don't intend to pay much attention. Abby, what are you doing?"

"Someone forgot the chair," Abby said.

Matthew pushed his hat back and then flopped down in the rocker, settling in as though he had just finished a hearty meal. "So kind of you to give me a ride," he said.

"Matthew." Abby felt desperate. "This is no time for joking. Please, get up. We're too far behind. Emma may need me."

Matthew stood up. "We can't take the chair any farther, Abby. We'll never get it over the mountains."

Abby shook her head. "Would you leave your gun? Would I leave my watch?"

"Of course not—but that's different. We can't survive without the gun. And the watch takes no space."

Abby took her makeshift harness in hand and tugged at the strings, her body leaning into the pull. "This chair means as much to Emma as your gun means to you," she said firmly.

"You Parkers are certainly stubborn," Matthew called from behind. "If you'd slow down, I'd help you."

Abby ignored him. If she had to speak again, her throat might close up. She followed the wagon for an hour or more, keeping a safe distance. Occasionally, when the oxen stopped to breathe, Abby poked her head inside. "All right?" she said. When Emma whispered a weak yes, Abby dropped back again, pulling the chair alone. Matthew went to relieve Will with the oxen while Abby slipped behind, her legs and body wasted with exhaustion. The wagon creaked dismally in the distance. What if they left her to die beneath these cold, unfeeling stars? Would anyone notice—or mind?

The sky lightened, and Abby watched the moon sink lower into the clouds. Gray mounds rose on the horizon. Were those the craggy hills of the desert—or the Sierras, at last?

"Matthew!" she cried. "Look at the mountains!"

As if they understood her, the oxen quickened their pace and bellowed. "They smell water!" Will called from the front of the wagon.

Abby tilted her head back, drawing a deep breath.

She coughed. All she could smell was manure and dust. She forgot the weight of the chair; she saw, instead, how the barren ground was now pockmarked with sage and greasewood. She saw a shrub, then another; heard voices, smelled smoke—and then a wrenching, agonized scream cut across the desert's edge.

Abby ran. Mother, please come back, she prayed as she clambered up into the wagon, her teeth chattering. Emma lay still as death on the thin pallet, the skin stretched tight over her high cheekbones. Her dark eyes were deep with fear and her hands made bunches of the torn blanket.

"Is it here?" Abby asked. She was afraid to draw the blanket back, afraid of what lay beneath. "I'll get Uncle Joseph—and find Mother—"

"No!" Emma gasped. "I don't want him here. He's too upset—that's why he screamed at you—" She groaned and tossed her head from side to side, as though fighting a nightmare. "Send for Mary. And don't leave me."

Abby crawled to the front of the wagon, where Will and Matthew were uncoupling the oxen, throwing nervous glances in her direction. "Will! Where's Uncle Joseph?"

Her brother wrenched the yoke over the horns of the lead ox and dropped it on the ground. "Gone to find Mother."

"Will, you've got to look for her too! Hurry—and bring us some water—please, hurry!" Abby was nearly sobbing; she lurched back into the wagon and stared helplessly at her aunt. What should she do?

Emma opened her eyes. "Come closer," she whispered. "Take my hand."

Abby obeyed, kneeling at her aunt's shoulders in the tiny space between the pallet and their jumbled belongings.

"Abby, did you watch animals give birth back home?"

"Of course. Lambs and calves—but Emma, this is different. We need Mother. I'm sure she'll be here in a minute."

"It's not so different." Emma gasped with pain again; when it passed, she wet her lips. "If only we had some water. Abby, you've got to know what to do." Her eyes pleaded for help.

Emma was right. Abby had no choice. As if someone were directing her, she helped Emma turn onto her side and pulled off her wet dress and chemise. Emma's belly rippled and hardened. Abby yanked the blanket over her and tried to focus her thoughts. What would they need? Something to keep the mattress dry—were there any flour bags left? She pawed through the mess beside her until she found some, wadded up beneath a trunk. Flannel, to wipe off the baby, she thought, remembering Suzy's birth: how the calf struggled for breath and Pa wiped her muzzle with a rag, freeing the velvet nostrils.

Abby made a neat pile next to the bed, then caught her breath. "Oh no—what about the cord?" she said softly. How would they cut it? She pulled Pa's heavy knife from her pocket. They'd need water to clean the blade. "Mother, please come," Abby whispered to herself. "I can't do this alone."

As if in answer to her prayers, a shaft of gray light fell across her face, and Mary Parker appeared, her head and shoulders framed in early morning light.

"Mother!" Abby cried. "The baby's almost here!"

Mary Parker climbed into the wagon with a pail of water in her hands and looked around. "I see you've thought of everything." She slipped her arm under Emma's shoulders. "Help me lift her up," she said, as though she and Abby had delivered countless babies together.

Emma groaned; the sound seemed to rise from the ground beneath the wagon before it was torn from her mouth. Mother held a cup of water to her lips and let Emma drink, then passed the cup to Abby.

"Push," Mary Parker urged, raising Emma by the shoulders. Abby supported her other side, and for countless minutes—maybe hours—the three of them moved up and down in waves, lifting Emma's heavy body as she bore down, releasing her to lie, panting and sweating, on the pallet when the contraction had passed. At some point, Matthew brought them more water and they all drank deeply; still later, Molly stuck her head in and spoke quietly, her eyes darkening. "Mr. Parker wonders, is everything all right?" she said softly.

"Of course it is," Mother answered. "Tell him we'll have a baby within the hour. And here—take Abby's pocketknife and wash it."

Molly disappeared. When she returned with the clean knife, Mother laid it on the flannel and whisked Molly away, closing the canvas behind her. Abby knew Molly felt left out, but there was no time to worry about that. Emma was straining again, her face clenched tight with the effort.

Suddenly Emma gave a violent cry; her body shook and she tossed from side to side on the pallet. "I can't do it!" she screamed. "Let me die. I'm too young to be a mother. I can't have this baby. Let me die, please."

"Nonsense," Mother said. She dipped a clean rag into the bucket of water and placed it between Emma's lips. "Suck on this." She pulled the blanket back and inched to the foot of the pallet.

Abby stroked her aunt's clammy forehead. "We've reached the Sierras," she said softly. "The baby made it all the way from Ohio to California. You can't give up now."

"Abby's right," Mother said. "One more push."

Emma took a deep breath and lunged forward; the wagon shuddered.

"There's the head." Mother's voice was flat, matter-of-fact. "Now wait—all right, *push!*"

Abby watched, in awe, forgetting Emma's modesty, as a small, bloody form slithered out onto the flour sacks. There was a tiny, choking sound, like the sneezing bleat of a newborn lamb, and then an astonished cry as Mary Parker slapped the baby's round bottom and deftly wiped its face with a cloth.

"The knife, please, Abigail," she said.

As her mother cut the cord, Abby leaned over Emma, who had fallen back on the pallet, too weak to raise her head. "It's a girl," Abby whispered, "with beautiful dark hair, like yours." She pried the watch from Emma's fingers and snapped it open. "Born at eight-fifteen in the morning, in the shadow of the Sierra Nevada mountains."

"What happened?" Uncle Joseph's anxious face appeared at the front of the wagon. Abby inched forward and smiled, her anger forgotten. "Uncle Joseph," she crowed. "It's a girl!"

Her uncle blinked and wiped his face quickly with the back of his hand. "Is she all right—is Emma all right?"

"I'm fine," Emma whispered. "I had two wonderful midwives." She squeezed Abby's hand. "Thank you," she said. "You got me through."

Abby smiled at Uncle Joseph. He pulled her into an awkward embrace. "Forgive me," he said. "I was beside myself with worry." He released her and cleared his throat.

"It's all right," Abby said. "I'm sure it's sometimes hard to have *me* for a niece."

"Not today," he said gruffly. He leaned into the wagon. "Emma," he said. "Abby did something else for you." He caught his breath and began to laugh, almost sobbing with deep, broken gulps.

"What is it?" Emma asked, turning her head to look at him.

"She hauled your chair all the way from the sink-hole," he said.

"Abby," Emma cried softly. "I thought it was gone for good."

"How else would you feed the baby?" Abby asked.

"She could use a little breakfast now," Mother said, and handed the infant, red and squalling, to Emma. "What will you call her?"

"Rebecca," Emma said in a clear voice. She held the baby to her breast and peered at the tiny face. "Rebecca, for my mother. Nevada for the mountains, Parker for the family she's born into. Rebecca Nevada Parker. Welcome to the world."

September 14, 1850.

Dearest Caroline,
Rebecca Nevada Parker was born on September 3, near the Great Meadows. I assisted at the birth. Emma is very weak, so we've been moving slowly to let her rest. We stayed at the meadows three days to cut hay for the animals, then climbed along the Truckee River toward the mountains.

Uncle Joseph is worried that snow will come before we reach the pass. We've heard there are soldiers coming east with supplies to help the last of the travelers over the summit, so Uncle Joseph sent Frank Watson ahead to look for a rescue party. We hope they find us before we run out of food. No one wants to eat our poor oxen, who nearly died hauling us across the desert.

Do you notice the date? It's my fifteenth birthday. I've changed a lot since we left Ohio last spring! There were no presents, of course, but Uncle Joseph gave me a sip of brandy from his emergency flask, and Mother spoiled me by sending me away while she made a noon meal from our meager supplies. When I came back, Will and Matthew surprised us with two trout they had caught in the river. That was a birthday treat for everyone. We managed to have a festive lunch; Will even spoke nicely to Molly, and Emma sat up in her rocker with the baby.

The Truckee is a fine river for my collection. It cuts a deep gorge through the dry hills. When no one was looking today, I took a birthday swim in an icy whirlpool that spun me around beneath the pine trees. Tomorrow we'll continue up the long canyon toward the Sierras. They look like the roof of the world.

Let's pray my next letter is written at the Yuba River,
Your affectionate sister,
Abigail

September 17. Truckee Pass.

Abby leaned against a boulder to catch her breath. She'd been climbing for an hour or more, hoping to find Frank Watson and a rescue party coming back over the pass. But the trail switched back on itself, crisscrossing the jagged peak from one side to the other, until Abby felt as if she were always in the same spot. Below her, in the dry valley where they'd spent the night, Donner Lake gleamed like a dark teardrop. If Abby peered over the rim of the trail, she could see the small figures of her family, creeping forward with agonizing slowness as they wrenched their last wagon over the boulders.

Abby opened her watch. Noon. Should she wait for the others? She tried to forget the cup of rice and the pinole cake she shared with Molly last night. It might be days before they ate again.

The sky darkened and a fine drizzle began to fall. Abby started uphill again when she heard a gunshot, followed by a man's hoarse scream. She held her breath, praying it was only the wind shrieking as it had last night. But these were human sounds, dark cries interspersed with reports from a rifle.

Abby turned and slithered back down the trail it had taken her so long to climb. Panic drove her faster; she rounded a boulder and hurtled headlong into her brother. Will clutched Abby with one hand, grabbing a scrawny tree with the other.

"What happened?" Abby cried. Her brother's jacket

was in shreds, one pant leg was torn at the knee, and his bloodshot eyes, oozed with a nameless emotion. He tried to speak, then covered his face with his hands.

"What's *wrong?*" Abby tugged desperately at his jacket. An acrid taste burned in her throat.

"Abby. Stop." Matthew came around the bend, out of breath. His eyes were dim in his gaunt face.

"Matthew, something awful's happened. Is it Mother?"

Matthew shook his head and gripped her shoulders. "Steady," he said, running an index finger gently across her forehead. "Your uncle's been killed."

A cold numbness settled in the pit of Abby's stomach. Matthew's arms were around her before she knew she was sobbing; he held her tight and she gave in to his steady warmth. If only she could cling to his jacket forever, steeped in the dank, reassuring odor of smoke and oxen.

"What do you mean, killed?" she asked at last, her voice rising to an unfamiliar pitch.

Will's speech was thick and strange. "Uncle Joseph saw an animal. Called it a marmot. He stopped to take aim. Someone shot Chester out from under him." Will's sigh was like the wind, sucking in its breath across the ravine. Two angry spots pulsed beneath his eyes. "He was so close to the edge—he just toppled over. I watched him bounce down the mountain."

"Who shot him?" Abby whispered.

"I don't know. I couldn't see anyone. I took a few shots into the woods, to scare him—" Will's voice broke. "Guess he got away. God knows what he wanted."

"A horse to eat," Matthew said grimly. "Maybe he saw the marmot. Everyone's starving."

Abby patted Will's back with her open palm and waited for him to stop shaking. "Where's Uncle Joseph now?"

"I went after him," Will said. "Matthew kept one end of a rope, I took the other. Don't know how I got down." He turned his palms up, staring in a stupefied way at the welts. "I tied the rope to his waist. Matthew and Timothy hauled him up. His neck was broken." Will hung his head. "If only he'd been in the middle of the trail with me."

"It's not your fault," Abby said fiercely. An angry, piercing wail floated up from the rocks below. "Emma!" Abby gasped.

"We'd better go down," Matthew said, pressing Abby's hands. "She's beside herself. Won't let us touch the body." He sighed. "I liked your uncle, even though he didn't make it easy."

Matthew pushed the hair back from his forehead. Somehow the familiar gesture propelled Abby forward. "Come on," she said, yanking Will's sleeve. "Let's hurry."

They stumbled in a drunken line down the path, clutching each other for comfort as much as for balance. Guilty thoughts scuttled in and out of Abby's mind like crabs on a dry riverbank. She'd often hated Uncle Joseph. When he scolded her in front of everyone, she'd even wished he were dead. But he was only taking care of them, as he'd promised Pa. Now she could never apologize.

She tripped and felt the steadying grasp of Matthew on one side, her brother on the other. She thought of her uncle standing up for the women at the Humboldt Sink, and the awkward way he hugged her when Rebecca was born. We *did* forgive each other, she thought. And then she remembered watching the Kansas River swirl past—so long ago now, it might have been the beginning of her childhood—and Emma saying bitterly, "Gold fever makes a man crazed."

They rounded a massive boulder and came face to face with Molly, who sat slumped against a wagon wheel, her head between her knees. Mary Parker stood beside her, jostling Rebecca up and down on her shoulder. The baby was howling, each anguished cry winding down to a watery trilling. In the middle of the trail, Emma lay prostrate over the still body of her husband.

"Emma," Abby said, bending over to touch her shoulders.

Her aunt rose to her knees, pulling at Abby's dress with frantic, childlike tugs. Her face was swollen and distorted. "Abby, I can't go on. God has forsaken us."

Bewildered, Abby turned to her mother for help, but Mary Parker stared right through her. Abby stroked her aunt's head to quell her own fear. "Emma, you can't give up now. Listen to Rebecca. She needs you."

Emma shook her head. "*Look* at him," she sobbed.

Abby forced her eyes to the ground. Uncle Joseph's chin jutted forward, as firm in death as in life, and his eyes bulged like someone awakened from a nightmare. His lips were pulled back over his teeth in a grimace, and his head lolled on the ground at an awkward angle. Abby knelt on the stones. She couldn't bear those eyes. Nausea crept into her throat, but she ignored it. Her stomach was empty anyway. With trembling fingers, she pulled one taut eyelid down and then the other, closing the lamps in her uncle's face forever.

As if Abby's gesture had released something inside her, Emma stopped weeping. She bent over her husband and kissed his forehead. When she began to whisper in his ear, Abby stepped aside, ashamed to witness such a private moment.

The wind moaned like someone sobbing. Emma climbed into the wagon and came out swinging Uncle Joseph's gold pan high above her head. She hurled it into the abyss with a wrenching howl.

"Stop!" Matthew cried as Emma flung a bundle of clothing over the rocks. Uncle Joseph's jacket and pants drifted through emptiness, billowing out until Abby had the brief, hideous sense of reliving her uncle's fall.

"Abby." Mother spoke for the first time, her voice tight and controlled. "Take the baby." Abby held Rebecca in her arms and waited for Mother to tell her what to do next. But she turned without a word and began to climb slowly up the trail, her back set straight.

"Mother!" Abby called. "Where are you going?" Her mother never looked back. Her tiny figure grew smaller, and she disappeared around a bend in the trail.

Rebecca squirmed in Abby's arms, her head twisting like an eager bird toward Abby's chest. "She's hungry," Abby said, frantically searching the group for a response. But Will stood frozen. Molly's head was still buried in her skirts; her spindly arms clutching her knees. Emma, climbing down from the wagon on Matthew's arm, stared vacantly into space.

Matthew whistled, a low, mournful sound. When Abby caught his eye, a look of understanding passed between them. Everyone else had given up. They were in charge now.

For days afterward, Abby remembered little of that endless afternoon. She knew that somehow Matthew had persuaded Will to help him load Uncle Joseph in the wagon, that Molly had walked numbly beside Timothy, holding onto Emma's leg to keep her from toppling off. She remembered the broken look on Emma's face when they found a flat place to lay Uncle Joseph down, her screams when they rolled stones over his body. But Abby had no idea how they managed to winch the wagon up the endless pitch, or whether she had ever found a way to quiet Rebecca's sobbing.

At the height of land, where the wind howled and mountains fell away in dark, brooding ridges, someone had propped a crude sign against the rocks. Mary Parker was waiting there for them, staring coldly at the letters scribbled in faded charcoal. TRUCKEE PASS, it said. Abby thought of her own sign, painted so long ago. She'd been full of hope and enthusiasm then. Now she moved in a dream, drained by lack of food and worn so close to the bone she couldn't even grieve.

Darkness rushed over them, spilling down from the peaks. Abby and Matthew urged everyone forward through windswept heights onto a vast plateau, thick with pines. They tried to build a fire, but the wood was wet. In the end, Abby and Matthew took turns standing watch while the others huddled in their damp bedrolls.

When Abby lay down, long after midnight, she twisted and squirmed, trying to avoid the roots. She clenched her fists in her ears to shut out the sound of Emma's crying, and fell into a dream where Uncle Joseph hurtled down an endless spiral.

Sometime close to dawn, Abby woke to Matthew's light touch on her sleeve. She sat up stiffly and looked into his face. Deep circles rimmed his eyes, and a stubble of beard accentuated the hollows beneath his cheekbones. He's right; we're starving, she thought. Out loud, she said, "You didn't wake me."

"No. I fell asleep," he whispered.

Abby scrambled out of her bedroll. A thin layer of wet snow clung to the boughs of the trees. She took a step; soft hunks matted under her moccasins. "Snow," she breathed quietly. "Matthew, we've got to get help."

"I know," he said. "Emma's sick; nearly mad with grief. Your mother and Molly are too weak to travel. Will can care for the others while we're gone. He can kill the oxen, one at a time. That will keep them going a few days, maybe longer."

Abby tried not to think about the members of the Donner party, whose ghosts seemed to hover over the pass. "What if we can't get back?" she whispered.

"We will," Matthew said. "Frank Watson's just ahead, I'm sure of it. He'll show up with a rescue party."

Abby ignored the false hope in his voice. Who was he fooling? But she stumbled to the wagon and climbed in. Emma's blank eyes stared at the canvas, and she shook from head to foot.

"Milk fever," Mother said. She sat up slowly, her hollow face pleading. Abby clasped Mother in her arms. She was so thin! Like delicate whalebone, curved around air.

Mother gave Abby a small pack. "Don't cry. Your things are in here," she said. "Wear my boots. I'll use Joseph's."

Inside, Abby felt relief. Mother was weak, but something—perhaps Emma's illness—had jolted her out of yesterday's despair.

"Take your bedroll," Mother continued. "You may be gone a few days."

Or forever, Abby thought desperately. Rebecca whined and fretted beneath the blanket.

"We're counting on you," Mother whispered. "You can make it." She reached beneath her mattress and drew out a small leather pouch. "For Matthew. In case of emergency."

Abby had to smile. "It's not an emergency now?"

Mother shook her head. "You've got more strength than you know," she said in a flat voice. "Now go. Take

Timothy. You can eat him, if need be."

Abby was shocked. She would *never* eat her pony. She tugged the leather boots onto her swollen feet, slipped the moccasins into her pack, and took a last, starved look at Mother's face. She kissed her, then touched her aunt's hot cheek.

"Goodbye, dear Emma," she said. Emma's eyes flickered, but she didn't answer. Abby ran her finger lightly over Rebecca's soft scalp and clambered down from the wagon.

The sun rose, melting the snow in the clearing. Molly stood gripping Matthew by the elbows, swaying as if she might faint. "You'll come back?" Abby heard her say.

"Of course." Matthew embraced her. Abby dusted the snow from Timothy's raw, matted hair. Matthew helped her to cinch their few possessions onto the pony's back while Will and Molly stood awkwardly to one side, keeping a careful distance between them.

"Ready?" Matthew asked. He kissed Molly again.

"Goodbye, Molly," Abby said, hugging her quickly. "Take care of Mother and Emma, if you can." She turned to Will. "Kill an ox," she said. "And make a fire. Everyone's cold." After all the months of resenting Will's orders, Abby felt strange, telling him what to do. She flung her arms around her brother. "We'll be back soon," she promised. "And Will—please be kind," she added in a whisper, nodding toward Molly.

Will spread his hands across her back and rubbed her shoulder blades. "I will," he said hoarsely.

Abby picked up Timothy's reins and followed Matthew down the trail, her boots leaving dark tracks in the snow.

September 21. On the western slope of the Sierra Mountains.

Late in the afternoon of the third day, Abby slumped against the rough bark of a pine tree. She rubbed her ears, trying to scrub away the buzzing sound, but it grew louder, like the rasping of a fiddle string bowed too hard. She was numbly aware of Matthew holding her hand, but she hardly noticed; all sensation focused on her empty stomach and the droning in her head.

The pony, pawing at the thin snow with dejected movements, whickered softly. Matthew raised his head and stared at Timothy with glittering eyes.

Abby knew what Matthew was thinking. "No," she said, stumbling to the pony and weaving her fingers in and out of the matted mane. "Not yet. Please wait. Tomorrow, we'll find something. A mouse. Pine nuts. We'll meet the rescue party." She leaned across Timothy's back. It was hard to get the words out.

"Maybe." Matthew was despondent. "What if Frank never made it out?"

"I don't know," Abby said. She knew things could

hardly be worse, but she didn't dare say that out loud. "Let's make camp," she said.

They made their preparations in silence; Matthew gathered branches for a fire while Abby cut pine boughs for a bed. The air was raw and cold; it settled heavily on the ground under the trees as the last of the daylight melted up to the crowns of the pines. Abby moved as if in sleep. She thought if she kept very still, focused on the inner core of her being, she might keep a slender hold on who she was. But the buzzing began again when she leaned over to place her branches on the ground. She watched the whirling earth and Matthew's sunken eyes approach her with the same deadly speed. A great howling roar filled her head, and the spinning became a wheeling vortex that sucked her into the dark.

Someone called her name from Truckee Pass, from the Bear River, from the Platte. She resisted swimming up out of the black chasm that engulfed her. She was safe from hunger in that dark pit. But the calling persisted, and gradually Abby rose to the surface.

"Abby!" Matthew cried, rubbing her cheeks with his fingers. "What happened?"

Abby looked up. Her head was cradled in his lap. "There was a buzzing. . . ." She closed her eyes again, listening, but the sound was gone, leaving only a deep, empty hunger. "I can't go on," she said, slurring her words. "Leave me here. No point both of us dying."

Matthew covered her with his jacket and stood up. "Don't move," he said. "I'll be right back."

He was gone for a while, and Abby listened to the mournful whine of the wind shifting the trees. Her head felt light, detached. She dozed, and woke to the scent of strong fumes beneath her nose. Matthew tipped a flask to her lips. A few searing drops of liquid dribbled down her throat to burn with a tiny flame in her stomach.

Before she could ask where the flask had come from, Matthew capped it and held out the leather pouch Mother had given them for an emergency.

Abby tore it open and found a stained kerchief wrapped around two crusty corncakes and six shriveled rings of dried apple. Tears pricked Abby's eyes as she imagined Mother hoarding this precious food when she needed it herself. "Hold out your hand," she whispered, and placed one of the cakes delicately in Matthew's palm. They ate them greedily and then looked for a long time at the apples.

"Might as well eat them, too," Matthew said at last. "We'll be hungry in the morning no matter what we do."

They chewed the hard, dry fruit carefully, as if each ring were a delicacy, and then Abby clambered to her feet, clutching Matthew's shoulder for support.

"Where are you going?" he demanded. "Save your strength."

Without an answer, she carried the bag to the fire and sat down, pouring the contents into her lap. Three letters fell out, along with the book that held her river collection. Mother had remembered the diary—how could Abby have forgotten it? She picked up the letters and turned them to the firelight. One was addressed to her, one to Matthew, and a third said: "In case of emergency, please deliver to William Parker, South Fork of the Yuba River, c/o Sutter's Fort, California."

Abby thrust Matthew's envelope into his hands and slit hers open, angling the pages toward the firelight. Mother's writing, usually so round and uniform, straggled across the page.

Dearest Abigail,
I pray you find the help we need to survive. If not, go on to the mines and look for your father. We shall find strength to continue or join our brother Joseph in heaven.

You have given me much joy since your birth. Though I have tried to curb your spirit, I believe your zest for life is your greatest strength. May it guide you in these troubled days.

If we don't meet again in this life, we shall be united in the next. You have my prayers for many long and happy years. If your later life includes Matthew Reed, you have my blessings.

Your devoted mother,
Mary Constance Parker

For the first time in days, Abby felt a rushing surge of hot temper. She jumped to her feet and stamped the ground with her boot.

Matthew chuckled. "Feeling better?"

"Mother talks as if we're all going to die." Abby

stalked up and down in the dark, shaking Mother's letter at the fire. "She thinks it's finished. Well, I have news for you, Mother!" she shouted. "We're not giving up now." The wind sighed in the pines, as if to carry her quavering message back along the high plateau to the wagon.

Abby rubbed her watch and thought about Pa. If he was still alive, he'd be waiting, worrying. Somehow, they'd make it to the Yuba River.

"What does she say to you?" Abby demanded.

"Kind things. If we wish to marry, she approves."

"Well, don't worry," Abby snapped. "You're free to do whatever you want. And so am I."

"Maybe I want to marry you."

Abby found his eyes and held them briefly. Then she clenched her fists. "Matthew, I'm only fifteen! We're alone in the mountains, with no help in sight. My family's scattered all over California. We have to *survive*."

Matthew laughed. "I don't hear you refusing. And you may be fifteen in years, but we're both older in other ways. We've been through a lifetime since Independence."

Abby drew her shawl close around her. "Don't make me think about it now. We need every bit of strength for tomorrow. We'll find help then. I know it."

Matthew drew close, until his face nearly touched hers. "Your mother's hand was shaking when she wrote," he said, "but she still scolded me, reminding me to behave like a gentleman." His teeth shone briefly in the firelight. "That means no more than this." He kissed her quickly. "I may not look or smell like a gentleman, but I'll do my best to behave."

"Behaving was never one of my strong points." Abby smiled and returned his kiss, standing on tiptoe to reach his mouth. Matthew held out his hands, but she stepped back, suddenly shy. "We'd better try to sleep," she said.

With slow, tired movements they fed the fire, tended to the pony, and carried their bedrolls to a heap of cut pine boughs. They spread their blankets as they had each night: with plenty of space between them. Lying still, with mist wetting her cheeks, Abby was acutely aware of Matthew's breathing. She'd just had a proposal of marriage—did he think she'd turned him down? Something stirred inside, a hot quickening deep in her belly that was separate from hunger, or perhaps hunger of a different kind, equally unsatisfied. Abby drifted into an uneasy sleep.

Hours later, she woke to a cocoon of warmth pressed against her back. Matthew had drawn his bedroll close to hers; he slept with an arm thrown over her shoulder and his head tucked into the nape of her neck. Abby lay still, enjoying the feel of his long legs against her own, even with the layer of blanket between. She thought of their ride over the prairie so many months ago, when Matthew's knees left a deep imprint on her spine. She'd been frightened then. Now she felt both a deep comfort and a craving. She waited for sleep to return, but her stomach began to gnaw. In another hour, the trees emerged from the fog. Abby stiffened and held her breath. Voices!

She wriggled out of her blankets and stood up, begging her weak legs to support her.

"What is it?" Matthew groaned.

"Listen!" Abby cried. "Someone's on the trail. Coming from the west."

Timothy snorted and pawed the ground, his ears flicking back and forth. Matthew grabbed his gun and lurched to his feet. Distant hooves clattered on rock. Abby and Matthew stumbled to the edge of their clearing.

"Careful," Matthew whispered. "Don't show yourself. Think of Uncle Joseph."

Abby's heart pounded in her throat. She peered anxiously into the fog. A mule's nose emerged from the mist, his back laden with supplies. Behind him, on sturdy pack ponies, was a short line of soldiers in heavy blue coats.

"A rescue party!" Abby cried. She ran from the clearing and stood shivering in the middle of the trail, her eyes streaming.

The lead rider pulled up in front of her, and a soldier jumped down. His face was hidden by a thick scarf, but his brown eyes were kind beneath his hat brim. "Are you all alone, miss?" he asked.

Abby shook her head and pointed in Matthew's direction. She was shaking with sobs, unable to speak. Relief, combined with the sickening worry about her family, flooded her in waves.

The soldier yanked a blanket from his saddlebag and draped it over her shoulders. "My God," he exclaimed. "You're just a girl—not much older than my own daughter. Who *are* you?"

Matthew took a step forward and emerged from the fog. "She's Abigail Reed. I'm Matthew Parker."

Abby's sobs became a thick laughter that nearly choked her. "You've mixed up our names," she said to Matthew when she could catch her breath.

Matthew shifted his feet with embarrassment, but the soldier smiled and shook their hands. "Captain Johnson, U.S. Cavalry," he said. "Parkers or Reeds, whichever you are, your loyal friend Frank Watson told us all about you. He made us promise we'd come after you."

"Is he all right?" Matthew asked.

The captain nodded. "We sent him on to Sutter's Fort to recuperate." His eyes flickered with concern. "But he mentioned seven people and an infant—"

Before he could finish his sentence, Abby and Matthew began speaking at once. In a garbled jumble of words they spilled out the story of Uncle Joseph's death, the family's hunger, their own harrowing days alone in the woods, crawling west. Finally Captain Johnson held up a hand. "Steady, now. You can tell us the whole story soon. Sounds like we need to hurry." He hesitated and looked from Abby to Matthew. "Are you brother and sister?"

Abby blushed, reading his thoughts. "No—my

brother's with the others. Matthew's just—a friend," she said.

"We were the only ones strong enough to go for help," Matthew added quickly.

"Never mind," the soldier said kindly. "No one worries about propriety at a time like this." He ordered the soldiers to dismount and took them aside. Although Abby couldn't hear what they were saying, she guessed, from their glances, that they were trying to decide what to do with her. She reached deep inside for the strength Mother promised she'd have, knowing she'd be all right if she could only have something to eat. She gripped the soldier's pony with one hand to steady herself.

Captain Johnson returned. "Where are you headed?" he asked.

"The South Fork of the Yuba River."

He turned to Matthew. "And you?"

"We're together," Matthew said simply.

Abby couldn't look at him, remembering all he'd said last night. "My pa's waiting for us," she said to the soldier. "William Parker. You know him?"

The captain shook his head. "Afraid not. Thousands of miners arrive every day. I know the area, though. Tell you what. How about letting one of my men escort you to Sutter's Fort? There are women there who can care for you until your family arrives. Your friend can show us where you left the others—"

"No, thank you," Abby said firmly. "I can make it. Besides, my family needs me. We'll finish this trip together."

"Abby's not going anywhere without me," Matthew added.

The captain pulled off his scarf and grinned. "Two people with fixed minds. Well, I'm sure you're right, miss. Your family's probably lost without you in more ways than one, if you'll pardon my poor humor. Let's get you something to eat. And if you don't mind dressing like a man, we'll loan you some clothes. You look mighty cold."

A few hours later, well fed and dressed in cavalry breeches and jackets, Abby and Matthew rode behind Captain Johnson on fresh, lively ponies. When the sun broke through the fog, Abby felt it was a lucky omen. Even Timothy—rescued from the soldier's guns by Abby's pleas—walked with a jaunty step, his belly full of oats.

Midway through the next day, Abby spotted her family's wagon inching toward them through the trees. She whooped, kicked her horse to a canter, and careened forward, counting figures. She was shrieking their names before she reached them: "Mother! Will! Emma! Molly! You're safe!"

She tumbled off the horse, nearly falling flat on her face, and lunged toward her mother. Mary Parker grasped Abby with trembling hands. Tears streamed unchecked down her weathered face.

"*Abby,*" Mother said in a lost voice, the name sounding like a prayer. "Dear child, I never thought I'd see you again." Mother gathered Abby to her. In a moment, she was crushed; Will, Molly, Matthew, Emma, and the baby were tangled together, with Mother lost in the middle. It was a long time before anyone could speak. When they'd hugged each other and drawn apart, grasping for words, Mother straightened her shoulders almost invisibly beneath her tattered dress. She tried to glare at her daughter through her tears.

"Abigail," she said sternly. "Where did you find those wretched trousers?"

Will's hoarse laugh sounded first; the others joined him until no one knew where the crying ended and the laughter began. At last, Mary Parker held up her hand for quiet and smiled at the captain, who was waiting just beyond their circle, his own face wet with tears. "You saved us."

"Thank your daughter and her friend," the soldier said quietly. "They found us."

Mother nodded. "I'll do that." She gave Matthew a quick kiss and stroked Abby's hair. Abby tucked her head onto Mother's bony shoulder, realizing, with a start, how small her mother seemed. She was amazed to think she could have grown taller while eating so little.

"You know what?" Mother was saying, approaching Captain Johnson. "I believe we could *all* use some of those pants, if you can spare them. What do you say, Emma? Molly? Will? Let's finish the journey in style."

October 10, 1850. Nicolaus, California.

Dearest Caroline,

A quick letter before we board a steamship that will carry us to the port of Marysville, near Yuba City. The ragged, nearly starved remains of your family came over the Sierras with the help of a rescue party, sent east from Sutter's Fort to round up the last of the "Golden Migration." We're all together but two—Uncle Joseph is buried near the pass, and we still have no news of Pa.

Captain Johnson, who led us down the last, steep descent of the mountains, wanted us to go with him to Sutter's Fort. Mother was tempted, but Will and I persuaded her to move on toward the Yuba River. We will send the captain off with messages of thanks for Frank Watson, as well as our packets of letters to you.

It will be wonderful to sit and let the engines do the work of moving us. After weeks alone in the mountains, when we thought we'd never see another soul, it's almost a comfort to be back in a crowd. There are few women here, and we have to laugh when miners look our way—Molly says they must be desperate, to fasten their eyes on us!

No matter where we end up, Matthew and Molly will stay with us through the winter. We're bound together by the journey. The whistle is blowing—I wish I could write more. Things have happened that I'll never forget, as long as I live. But I'm still your devoted sister,

Abigail

October 15, 1850. Yuba River.

Abby huddled in her damp bedroll, dreaming she was throwing horseshoes against their barn in Ohio. When the clanging grew louder, she opened her eyes. Outside their sagging canvas roof, Matthew's long legs were braced wide as he pounded a stake with the blunt end of an ax.

"Matthew!" Abby hissed, but he didn't hear; he slipped away through the mud. Abby stared at Molly's dark head, huddled in sleep beside her, then turned toward Emma. Her aunt was dozing; Rebecca lay in the crook of her arm, humming loudly as she nursed. Abby was about to say good morning when she heard her mother's voice. She pushed off her bedroll and sat up, listening.

"This is the end of the line for me," Mother said firmly.

Abby scrambled to her feet and stepped carefully over Emma and the baby, hiding herself in the shadows. Just outside the makeshift tent, Mother and Will were trying to start a fire in the rain. Mother coughed and fanned the smoke with her apron.

"I'm not going one more step. I've crossed this whole wretched continent for your father."

Will murmured a protest, but Mother answered coldly. "No. He's caused us enough hardship. Emma's too weak to move. We've no need to drag Matthew and

Molly on our own wild goose chase. It's time he came to find us."

Abby knew that when Mother gave one of her rare speeches, there was no way to budge her. But she sounded as though she'd lost her mind. Give up on Pa, *now?* Abby forgot all the times on the trail when she'd blamed Pa for their troubles, too; forgot the way she'd doubted whether he'd be there at all. She burst out from under the canvas. "Mother, how can Pa find us?" she blurted. "He doesn't even know we're here."

"He will, soon enough," Mother answered calmly. "I met an express man yesterday. He boasted he could find any miner in the state. I gave him a letter for your pa, telling him we'd wait here, in Nevada City. I'm sure he'll come before long."

Abby was shocked. "But Mother—we've already searched along the Yuba, and no one's heard of Pa—"

"He'll be upstream on one of the forks," Mother said. "The steamship captain told me that's where the gold is."

Abby thought about their slow trip up the Feather River from Nicolaus. As their boat plunged upstream and they regained their strength, Abby waited for Mother to take charge, but she was silent, her eyes fixed on the riverbanks. When Will used the last of their money to purchase provisions in Marysville, Mother mounted a fresh mule and followed obediently while they scoured the Yuba River for Pa, stopping at every shanty to shout his name above the roar of water.

Each time a stranger shook his head, Abby watched Mother's face tighten, as if a cord were cinching her neck. All that time, Abby assumed her mother had lost hope. In fact, she realized now, she must have been simmering with rage.

"We can't live in this wretched place," Mother said. "I'm going to find us a house. I'll be back by noon." She set off down the road, picking her way through the mud.

"She's too weak to go alone," Will said, starting after her, but Abby held him back.

"Wait," she said. "Mother's wrong. We can't stay here."

"*She* can," Will said. "I'll find Pa myself, if I have to."

"I'm coming with you," Abby said, expecting him to disagree, but he surprised her.

"Good. We'll check the town first. There must be a post office or a store where he'd come in to buy supplies."

They hurried away from camp. In a few minutes, they stood at the foot of the long, muddy hill that formed the town's main street, buttoning their coats against the drizzle. "Let's split up," Abby said. "We can each take one side of the street."

Will shook his head. "It's too rough. You can't be alone."

Abby laughed. "Really, Will. After everything that's happened? If anyone bothers me, I'll find you."

Before he could protest, she was jumping the rivulets

in the road. "First one to the top of the hill wins!" she called. Will shrugged, then suddenly gave a thumbs-up sign, accepting her challenge. He disappeared into the first doorway.

For half an hour, Abby went into a string of makeshift shops, her fingernails digging deep into her palms as she tried to ignore the lewd stares and whistles that greeted her arrival. She asked for her father in a shed where men sold mining equipment; she slipped into a tent full of chickens and asked a robust man if he'd met William Parker. Everywhere she went, men shook their heads.

Abby continued uphill, dazed by the cacophony of sound. Wagons rumbled past, groaning under enormous loads; saws rasped as buildings were tossed together. At the top of the street, a more permanent structure boasted a sign that said: ASSAY OFFICE. She climbed the porch steps and opened the door. A crowd of men turned their heads toward her in unison. Abby cringed and decided Will was right. Even in her borrowed trousers, she was clearly a woman.

She was about to slip away when she noticed an iron bank window at the front of the room. Behind the grating, a man wearing a green visor called out, "You're a sight for sore eyes!" He motioned her forward. Abby hesitated, wondering if she was safe, but the man smiled. "Don't worry—we haven't forgotten our manners, even if we hardly remember what a woman looks like."

Abby stepped up to the counter. The man was setting weights on one side of a scale, balancing them against a pile of glittering dust.

"Is that gold?" Abby asked breathlessly, forgetting the crowd.

The man nodded. "Pretty, ain't it? What can we do for you, miss?"

"I'm looking for my father—William Parker." Abby's words dropped like stones in the silent room.

The man thought a moment. "Parker," he said slowly. He leafed through an enormous ledger, scanning a list of names and figures with his index finger. "Nothing here." He raised his voice. "Any of you folks know a William Parker?"

The men murmured among themselves, then a burly man with a dark mustache stepped toward her. "Is he mining?"

"I guess so," Abby answered. "We've only had one letter."

"Count yourself lucky!" someone shouted, and everyone laughed. Abby looked down at her boots and flinched when the stocky man touched her shoulder.

"Come with me, miss," he said. "No need to be the center of attention." Outside on the narrow steps, he folded his arms over his chest. Abby studied his jacket; the pockets bulged and sagged with lumps. "There's a man named Parker up at Kanaka Creek," he said at last. "Near Downieville."

Abby's heart began to beat wildly in her throat, but she cautioned herself silently: Don't count on anything.

"He's running a supply business," the man continued. "Can you tell me what he looks like?"

Abby felt her cheeks burn with excitement. "He has dark red hair, like mine. And a beard, and he's—" She ran her eyes shyly over the man. "He's about your size," she said at last.

"Tells a good story?"

Abby nodded, scarcely daring to breathe. Couldn't there be hundreds of men who looked like her father, who attracted people with their exaggerated tales?

"I think he's the one," the man said, "though I can't promise. Reason is, he asks every stranger for news of his family. But Kanaka Creek's a far piece from here. You alone?"

Abby explained that her family was in town, trying to find a place to live; that her mother refused to move. Without thinking, she blurted, "But we can't stay here. Will—that's my brother—he and I are going to find Pa. Before winter comes."

"Of course," the man replied, reminding Abby of the trapper, who had accepted her quick decisions just as easily. "Tell you what. Soon as I turn in my rocks"—he patted his pockets—"I'm on my way to San Francisco. Got to bring in a boatload of supplies before the floods come. No one'll be in my cabin the next few weeks. We'll put your mother there. It's not much, just cowhide for walls, but it's snug. You wait here."

He went into the office. While she waited, an ugly worry slipped into Abby's mind. If it was Pa, why didn't he come looking for them?

She buried the thought when the man returned with a brown paper sack. He flattened it on his knee and sat down on the steps, drawing with a piece of charcoal. In a few minutes, a rough map took shape; Abby followed the curving lines as eagerly as if she were already riding up the winding mountain trail. When the man made a cross beside a curve in the creek, she almost snatched the paper from his hands. "*Thank* you," she said, smiling.

"My pleasure." He frowned. "Hope it's not a wild goose chase. If it is, you come back here. Ned Beame will help you." His face opened and Abby laughed, his smile was so like his name. When he explained the location of his cabin, Abby realized it was near their camp.

"I'll have Mother meet you there. She'll be so grateful."

"Think nothing of it, miss . . . Parker?"

"Abby."

"Righto." Mr. Beame shook her hand and said good-bye.

In the next hour, Abby found Will, dragged him breathlessly back to camp, and outlined her plan. They would leave before Mother came back, she explained, stuffing bundles of clothing into a saddlebag and taking a quick bite from a heel of bread. They would take the new mules; Timothy would stay in camp. As Abby talked, Emma watched in silence, holding the baby; Matthew shifted uneasily from one foot to the other.

Abby couldn't meet his eyes. Finally, Molly spoke.

"You should go," she said. "Your mother's been good to us. We'll take care of her, find Mr. Beame—won't we, Matthew?"

Before Matthew could answer, Will grabbed Molly's hand and shook it hard. "Thanks, Molly. You've been . . . kind. Not what I thought. I'm sorry for the way I treated you." He turned away, his face raw with embarrassment.

Molly's eyes filled with tears. "That's all right," she said.

Abby grabbed her bundles, but Matthew said "*Abby*" so forcefully that she stopped and looked into his eyes, held by their stillness.

"Abby, do you remember what I asked, our last night alone?"

"I guess," she teased. "Do you remember what I answered?"

"You didn't say no."

"Or yes. Matthew, come here." He followed her away from the camp. She turned to face him, rain streaking her face. "I've got plans I should tell you about."

His face paled, and she added quickly, "Silly. Not someone else. Ever since Pa wrote, I've known what I wanted here. A piece of land."

Matthew frowned. "Of your own? How would you do that? Where?"

"I don't know yet." Abby thought about the golden hills sprinkled with glossy live oak trees, slipping past the steamboat; about the deep canyons carved by the

Yuba River. "Matthew, the adventure's just begun. You'll have to be patient."

He laughed. "Abby, you weasel. Find your father. But come back."

"Of course I will." Abby kissed him. Will whistled sharply; they climbed on the mules and rode away without looking back.

In three days, they reached the head of the ravine drawn on their rough map. In the tiny settlement where the trail dropped to Kanaka Creek, Abby turned to her brother. "This is it," she said, feeling the blood pulse into her hands.

The trail was steep and slippery, gouged from the side of the mountain. Stones kicked aside by the mules tumbled into a deep gorge, hundreds of feet below. As they descended, the mountains stole the light and their pace seemed agonizingly slow. At the bottom of the canyon, the roar of water blended with the rhythmic pounding of picks and shovels. A group of Indians were building a flume, a long plank "table" beside the river.

Abby and Will peered anxiously into each face as they rode past. The men worked feverishly, as if racing the clouds gathered on the peaks. "Do you think this is it?" Will shouted above the noise.

Abby pointed and kicked her mule. Dead ahead of them, where the river took a sharp turn and disappeared, an enormous piece of canvas stretched like a roof above long tables. Abby jumped from the mule and

ran to the tent, jostling two miners. In the gloom beneath the canvas, she stumbled between tools and bags
of flour, then stood poised for a moment, like a cat
ready to spring. A man sat on a barrel, his hands slicing
the air. He was telling a story she knew by heart.

"So the old codger took that coon, whirled it three
times around his head, and flung it all the way to—"

"Heaven!" Abby called.

The man leaped to his feet as if he'd fallen on hot
coals.

"My God—"

"Pa!" Abby hurled herself against his burly chest.
"Pa!"

He staggered backward, caught himself, and laughed,
a deep roar that rumbled against her chest. "*Abigail.*"
His arms encircled her waist; they rocked against each
other for a long moment.

"Pa!" she crowed. "You're *alive.*"

"Just barely," he drawled. He held her at arm's
length. Abby drank in the long, scraggly beard; the
rusty thatch of hair, with more gray flecks than she remembered; the raw, deep scar scrawled across one temple.

"What happened?" Abby asked through tears, tracing
the scar with one finger. "What didn't you write us? We
thought you were dead."

"I was—almost," Pa said, his voice hoarse with feeling. "I know you must have wondered. Don't worry, I'll
explain everything."

He pushed her gently aside. Will emerged from the shadows, squinting in disbelief, his right hand outstretched.

"This is no time for a handshake!" Pa shouted, and swept him into his arms. "Look at this!" he cried to the astonished men in the tent, pounding Will's back. "My *family's* here." He released Will, took Abby's hand, and led them outside, his right leg swinging stiffly from his hip.

In the gray light beyond the canvas, Abby wiped her eyes and looked at her brother. Will's shoulders shook and his face crumpled as if he were small again. Pa searched the trail hungrily with his eyes.

Abby knew what he was thinking. "Mother's not here yet," she said quickly.

"Where is she?" Pa demanded, his mouth tight beneath his beard.

"In Nevada City," Will said, catching his breath. "She was too worn out to go any farther. And Pa . . ."

Abby helped him. "Uncle Joseph died. And his wife had a baby. Rebecca."

"One thing at a time." Pa's ruddy face had paled; he wiped his eyes with his sleeve and gazed deeply into their faces. "How did you find me?" he asked when he could speak again.

Abby explained about the man in Nevada City. "He wasn't the only one," she added. "People helped us everywhere."

"I left children behind. I see you're grown up now."

Pa cleared his throat. "Come on. I want to show you something."

As they walked along a narrow path, Abby dropped behind, noticing how Will's square back matched Pa's, how their wide hands made the same gestures as they talked. But Pa's gait, which she remembered as sturdy and brisk, was broken by the drag of his limp.

"Pa, what *happened* to you?" she asked.

He stopped and turned around. "I was building a Long Tom; that's a sluice for mining. A beam caught me in the head, dashed me into the rocks. Left me with this gash"—he drew a finger across his temple—"and smashed my leg. For months, I didn't know who I was, where I'd been." He waved at a small group of Indians who were building a dam. "Those Kanakas, from Hawaii, nursed me back to health. A few more weeks, I thought I could come find you. I just started walking without the crutch. I sent friends downstream, looking for you."

He cupped Abby's chin in his palm. His hazel eyes, so like her own, were wet. "You can't imagine how I felt when I came to myself and realized I didn't know where you were." He released her and pointed to the river. "Kanaka Creek's full of gold. Come spring, you might dig some up yourselves," Pa said, flashing a smile that stung Abby deep in her chest.

"Maybe." But Abby knew she'd already struck gold. All the way across the country, they had washed away the silt, sluicing themselves down to who they really were, the way a miner swirled his pan to clean sludge from the stones. Underneath our grit, there's burnished gold, Abby thought. It wasn't just Pa we found, crossing the country. It was ourselves.

"Here we are," Pa said. He stopped in front of a tiny cabin, nestled between towering pines and the stubbled hill. "It's ours. Think your mother will like it?" Abby could see the worry in his eyes. Pa must wonder, as she had, what it would be like when everyone was together.

"She'll like it," Will said. "She'll be a different person, with a roof over her head."

Abby knew he was right. Emma would feel the same way. As for herself, she could live outdoors forever.

Pa searched their faces. "The trip changes you, doesn't it?" When they nodded, he asked gently, "Was it worth leaving home—for this?"

Abby looked up the narrow canyon, its steep walls climbing to the sky like the insides of a bowl. "Oh, Pa," she laughed, hugging him. "We *are* home. Here on Kanaka Creek."